The Camp Fire Girls
At Sunrise Hill

Margaret Vandercook

1st WORLD
LIBRARY
Literary Society

The Camp Fire Girls At Sunrise Hill

Margaret Vandercook

© 1st World Library – Literary Society, 2004
PO Box 2211
Fairfield, IA 52556
www.1stworldlibrary.org
First Edition

LCCN: 2004091259

Softcover ISBN: 1-59540-677-8
eBook ISBN: 1-59540-777-4

Purchase *"The Camp Fire Girls At Sunrise Hills"*
as a traditional bound book at:
www.1stWorldLibrary.org/purchase.asp?ISBN=1-59540-677-8

1st World Library Literary Society is a nonprofit
organization dedicated to promoting literacy by:

- Creating a free internet library accessible from any computer worldwide.
- Hosting writing competitions and offering book publishing scholarships.

Readers interested in supporting literacy
through sponsorship, donations or
membership please contact:
literacy@1stworldlibrary.org
Check us out at: www.1stworldlibrary.org

The Camp Fire Girls At Sunrise Hill
contributed by the Charles Family
in support of
1st World Library Literary Society

CHAPTER I

THE VOICE

Betty Ashton sighed until the leaves of the book she held in her hand quivered, then she flung it face downward on the floor.

"Oh dear, I do wish some one would invent something new for girls!" she exclaimed, although there was no one in the room to hear her. "It seems to me that all girls do nowadays is to imitate boys. We play their games, read their old books and even do their work, when all the time girls are really wanting girl things. I agree with King Solomon: 'The thing that hath been, it is that which, shall be; and that which is done is that which shall be done; and there is no new thing under the sun.' At least not for girls!"

Then with a laugh at her own pessimism, Betty, like Hamlet, having found relief in soliloquy, jumped up from her chair and crossing her room pressed the electric button near the fireplace until the noise of its ringing reverberated through the big, quiet house.

"There, that ought to bring some one to me at last," she announced. "Three times have I rung that bell and yet no one has answered. Do the maids in this house actually expect me to build my own fire? I suppose I could do it if I tried."

She glanced at the pile of kindling inside her wood box and then at the sweet smelling pine logs standing nearby, but the thought of actually doing something for herself must have struck her as impossible, for the next moment she turned with a shiver to stare through the glass of her closed window, first up toward the sullen May sky and then down into her own garden.

Outside the gray clouds were slowly pursuing one another against a darker background and in the garden the lilacs having just opened their white and purple blossoms were now looking pale and discouraged as though born too soon into a world that was failing to appreciate them.

In spite of her petulance Betty laughed. She was wearing a blue dressing gown and her red-brown hair was caught back with a velvet ribbon of the same shade. Her room was in blue, "Betty's Blue" as her friends used to call it, the color that is neither light nor dark, but has soft shadows in it.

Betty herself was between fifteen and sixteen. She had gray eyes, a short, straight nose and her head, which was oddly square, conveyed an effect of refinement that was almost disdain. Her mouth was a little discontented and somehow she gave one the impression that, though she had most of the things other girls wish for, she was still seeking for something.

"The outdoors is as dismal as I am, no wonder we used to be sun worshipers," she said after a few more minutes of waiting; "but since Prometheus stole the fire from heaven some ages ago, I really don't see why I should have to freeze because the sun won't shine."

Frowning and gathering her dressing gown more closely about her with another impatient gesture, Betty swept out into the hall.

The house was strangely silent for the middle of a week-day afternoon; not a sound came either from below stairs or above, not the rattle of a window blind nor the echo of a single pair of footsteps.

At some time has a sudden silence ever fallen upon you with a sense of foreboding like the hour before a storm or the moment preceding some unexpected news or change in your life?

Betty hurried toward the back-stairs. She was leaning over the banisters and had called once for one of the maids, when she ceased abruptly, and stood still for several moments with her head tilted back and her body tense with surprise.

So long as Betty could recall, there had been a vacant room in the rear of the old Ashton homestead, which had stood for more than a hundred years at the comer of Elm Street in Woodford, New Hampshire. She was stupider than other people about remembering the events of her childhood and yet she was sure that this room had never been used for any purpose save as a storehouse for old pieces of furniture, for discarded pictures, for any odds and ends that found no other resting place about the great house. It was curious because the room was a particularly attractive one, with big windows overlooking the back garden, but then there was some story or other connected with it (old houses have old memories) and this must have made it unpopular. Betty did not know what the story was and yet she had grown up with a queer, childish dread of this room and rarely went into it unless she felt compelled.

Now, though she was not a coward, it did give her an uncanny sensation to hear a low, humming sound proceeding from this supposedly empty room.

Cautiously Betty stole toward its closed door and quietly turned the knob without making the least noise. Then she looked in.

What transformation had taken place! The room was a store place no longer, for most of the old furniture and all the other rubbish had been cleared away and what was left was arranged in a comfortable, living fashion. An old rug was spread out on the floor, a white iron bed stood in one corner with an empty bookshelf above it. There was a vase on a table holding a branch of blossoming pussy willow, and seated before one of the big, open windows was a strange girl whom Betty Ashton never remembered to have seen before in her life.

The girl was sewing, but this was not what kept Betty silent. She was also singing a new and strangely beautiful song.

"Lay me to sleep in sheltering flame, 0 Master of the Hidden Fire; Wash pure my heart, and cleanse for me My soul's desire."

Unconscious of the intruder and forgetful of everything else the singer's voice rose clearer and sweeter with the second verse.

"In flame of sunrise bathe my mind, O Master of the Hidden Fire, That when I wake, clear-eyed may be My soul's desire."

Then in silence, as she leaned closer to the window to get a better light on her sewing, an unexpected ray of sunshine managing at this moment to break through the clouds fell directly on her bowed head. Her hair was not auburn, like Betty's, but bright, undeniable red.

"That is a charming song and you have lovely voice, but would you mind telling me who you are, where you have come from and how you happen to be so at home in a room in our house?" Betty Ashton inquired, coolly, still keeping her position just outside the opened door.

The stranger jumped instantly to her feet, letting fall some brown embroidery silk and a number of bright-colored beads, then she stood with her eyes fixed anxiously on the apparition before her, nervously twisting her big, rather coarse-looking hands. She was a year older than Betty Ashton and at the first glance it would have been difficult to imagine two persons more unlike. Betty was slender but perfectly proportioned and had an air of unusual beauty and refinement, which her friends believed must come of her long line of distinguished ancestors, while the new girl was thin and angular, with hands and feet that seemed too big for her, and a pale, freckled skin. She too had gray eyes, but while Betty's brows and lashes were the color of her hair, this girl's were so light that they failed to give the needful shadows to her eyes.

In order to gain time and courage the newcomer walked slowly across the room, but when she spoke the beauty of her voice gave her unexpected charm and dignity.

"Hasn't your mother told you of my coming? didn't she ask you if you wanted me to come?" she questioned slowly. "I am sorry; my name is Esther Clark, but my name can mean nothing to you. Your mother has asked me here to live, to take care of your clothes, to read to you, to take walks when there is no one else - "

"Oh, you mean you are to be my maid," Betty finished, coming now into the center of the room and studying the other girl critically, her eyes suddenly dark with displeasure and her lips closed into a firm red line.

"I must say it is strange no one has thought to mention your coming to me, and as I am not a child, I think I might have been consulted as to whether I wished to be bothered with you." Betty bit her lips, for she did not mean to be unkind; only she was extremely provoked and was unaccustomed not to having her wishes consulted.

The older girl's face was no longer pale but had suddenly grown crimson. "No, I am not to be your maid," she returned. "At least Mrs. Ashton said I was to be a kind of companion; though I am to be useful to you in any way you like, I am still to go to school and to have time for studying. Of course the holidays are nearly here now, but later on I hope to graduate. If you don't wish me to stay you will please explain it to your mother, only - " Esther tried to speak naturally, but her voice faltered, "I hope you will be willing to let me stay at least until I can find some other place. I am too old to go back to the asylum."

"Asylum!" Betty stepped back in such genuine that her companion laughed, showing her white, even teeth and the softer curve to her mouth that relieved her face of some of its former plainness.

"Oh, I only meant the orphan asylum, so please don't be frightened," she explained. "I have lived there, it is just at the edge of town, ever since I was a little girl, because when my mother and father died, there was nothing else to do with me. But you need not feel specially sorry, because I have never been ill-treated in the fashion you read about in books. Most of the people in charge have been very kind and I have been going to school for years. Only when your mother came last week and said she wanted me to come here to live, why it did seem kind of wonderful to find out what a beautiful home was like, and then most of all I wanted to know you. You will think it strange of me, but I have been seeing you with your mother or nurse ever since you were a little girl of three or four and I a little older, and I have always been interested in you."

Betty smiled, showing a dimple which sometimes appeared after an exhibition of temper of which she felt ashamed. "Oh, you will be sorry enough to know what I am really like," she answered, "and will probably think I am dreadfully spoiled. But do please stay for a while if you wish, at least until we find how we get on together."

Since Betty's first speech at the door had startled her, Esther had never for a moment taken her eyes from her face. Never in all her life, even when she had seen and learned far more of the ways of the world, could this girl learn not to speak the truth. So now she slowly shook her head. "Your mother did say you were spoiled; it was one reason why she wished me to come here to live," she replied. "You see, she said that you had been too much alone and had too much done for you and that your brother was so much older that he only helped to spoil you. But," Esther was hardly conscious of her listener and seemed only to be thinking aloud, "I shall not mind if you are spoiled, for how can you help being when you are so pretty and fortunate and have all the things that other girls have just to dream of possessing."

It was odd, perhaps, but the new girl's speech was made so simply and sincerely that Betty Ashton instead of feeling angry or complimented was instead a little ashamed. Had fortune been kinder to her than to other girls, kinder than to the awkward girl in front of her in her plain gray linen dress?

Betty now backed toward the door which she had so lately opened. "I am sorry to have disturbed you, but usually this room isn't occupied and I was curious to know who could be in here. I should have knocked. Some day you must sing that lovely song to me, again, for I think I would like very much to know just what my soul's desire is. The worst of life is not knowing just what you want."

Esther had followed Betty toward the hall. "How funny that sounds to me," she returned shyly, "because I think the hard part of life is not having what you want. I know very well. But can't I do something for you now? Your mother said you were not well and perhaps would not wish to see me this afternoon, but I could read to you or - "

Betty's irritability returned. "Thank you very much," she returned coldly, "but I can think of nothing in the world that would amuse me at present. I simply wish not to freeze, and to save my life I can't get one of our tiresome maids to answer my bell."

Betty's grand manner had returned, but in spite of her haughtiness the newcomer persisted. "Do let me make the fire for you. I am only a wood-gatherer at present, but pretty soon I shall be a real fire-maker, for I have already been working for two months."

"A wood-gatherer and fire-maker; what extraordinary things a girl was forced to become at an orphan asylum!" Betty's sympathies were immediately aroused and her cheeks burned with resentment at the sudden vision of this girl at her side trudging through the woods, her back bent under heavy burdens. No wonder her shoulders stooped and her hands were coarse. Betty slipped her arm through the stranger's.

"No, I won't trouble you to make my fire, but do come into my room and let us just talk. None of my friends have been in to see me this afternoon, not even the faithless Polly! They are too busy getting ready for the end of school to think about poor, ill me." And Betty laughed gayly at the untruthfulness of this picture of herself.

Once inside the blue room, without asking permission, Esther knelt straightway down before the brass andirons and with deft fingers placed a roll of twisted paper under a lattice-like pile of kindling, arranging three small pine logs in a triangle above it. But before setting a match to the paper she turned toward the other girl hovering about her like a butterfly.

"I wonder if you would like me to recite the fire-maker's song?" she asked. "I haven't the right to say it yet, but it is so lovely that I would like you to hear it."

Betty stared and laughed. "Do fire-makers have songs?" she demanded. "How queer that sounds! Perhaps the Indians used to have fire songs long ago when a fire really meant so much. But I can't imagine a maid's chanting a song before one's fire in the morning and I don't think I should like being wakened up by it."

"You would like this one," the other girl persisted.

Little yellow spurts of flame were now creeping forth from between the sticks, some leaping away into nothingness, others curling and enfolding them. The paper in the grate crackled noisily as the cold May wind swept down the chimney with a defiant roar and both girls silently watched the newly kindled fire with the fascination that is eternal.

Betty had also dropped down on her knees. "What is your song?" she asked curiously an instant later, raising her hands before her face to let the firelight shine through.

Esther's head was bent so that her face could not be seen, but the beauty of her speech was reflected in the other girl's changing expression.

"As fuel is brought to the fire, So I purpose to bring My strength, my ambition, My heart's desire, My joy And my sorrow To the fire Of humankind."

Purposely Esther's voice dropped with these last words, and she did not continue until a hand was placed gently on her shoulder and a voice urged: "Please go on; what is the 'fire of humankind'?"

"For I will tend As my fathers have tended And my fathers' fathers Since time began, The fire that is called The love of man for man, The love of man for God."

At the end, Esther glancing around at the girl beside her was surprised to see a kind of mist over her gray eyes.

But Betty laughed as she got up to her feet and going over to her table stooped to pick up the book she had thrown on the floor half an hour before.

"I might have made my own fire if I had known that song," she said, switching on the electric light under the rose-colored shade. For the clouds outside had broken at last, the rain was pouring and the blue room save for the firelight would have been in darkness.

Betty sat down, putting her feet under her and resting her chin on her hands. "I wonder what it feels like to be useful?' she asked, evidently questioning herself, for afterwards she turned toward her companion. "You must have learned a great many things by being brought up at an orphan asylum, how to care for, other people and all that, but I never would have dreamed that poetry would have played any part in your education."

Esther had turned and was about to leave the room, but now at Betty's words, she looked at her strangely.

Her face had reddened again and because of the intensity of her feelings her big hands were once more pressed nervously together.

"Why, no, I never learned anything at the asylum but work," she answered slowly, "just dull, hateful, routine work; doing the same things over again every day in the same way, cooking and washing dishes and scrubbing. I suppose I was being useful, but there isn't much fun in being useful when nobody cares or seems to be helped by what you do. I know I am ugly and not clever, but I love beautiful people and, beautiful things."

Unconsciously her glance traveled from her listener's face to the small piano in the corner of the room. "And it never seemed to me that things, were divided quite fairly in this world, but now that I know about the Camp Fire, Girls I am ever so much happier."

"Camp Fire Girls?" Betty queried. "Do sit down, child, I don't wish you to leave me, and please don't say horrid things about yourself, for it isn't polite and you never can tell how things are going to turn out. But who are the Camp Fire Girls; what are the Camp Fire Girls; are they Indians or Esquimaux or the fire-maidens in 'The Nibelungen'? Perhaps, after all, something new has been invented for girls, and a little while ago I felt as discouraged as King Solomon and believed there was nothing new and nothing worth while under the sun."

Betty's eyes were dancing with fun and anticipation, her bored look had entirely disappeared, but the other girl evidently took her question seriously. She had seated herself in a small desk chair and kept her eyes fixed on the fire. "It seems very queer to me that you don't know about the 'Camp Fire Girls'," she answered slowly, "and it may take me a long time to tell you even the little bit I know, but I think it the most splendid thing that has ever happened."

CHAPTER II

"METHINKS YOU ARE MY GLASS"

Just across the street from the old Ashton place was another house equally old and yet wholly unlike it, for instead of being a stately, well-kept-up mansion with great rooms and broad halls and half an acre of garden about it, this was a cottage of the earliest New England type. It was low and rambling, covering a good deal of ground and yet without any porch and very little yard, because as the village closed about it and Elm Street became a fashionable quarter the land had been gradually sold until now its white picket fence was only a dozen feet from the front door and passers-by could easily have looked inside its parlor windows save for the tall bushes that served as a shield. By immemorial custom the cottage had always been painted white and green, but for a good many years it had not been troubled by any paint at all, "but had lived," as Polly said, "on its past, and like a good many persons in Woodford had gotten considerably run down by the process."

Now there were no lights at any of the front windows, although it was eight o'clock in the evening, but as the warm steady glow of a lamp shone from the rear of the house, it was plainly occupied.

There was no doubt of this in the mind of the girl who stood knocking noisily at the closed door, saying in an imploring voice:

"Oh, do please hurry, Polly dear, you know it is only me and that I can't bear to be kept waiting."

At this moment a candle was evidently being borne down the hall, for the door opened so quickly afterwards that two girls, one on either side the door, fell into, one another's arms.

"Dear me, it's 'The Princess' and she is no more ill than I am, though we were told she couldn't possibly be at school to-day on account of her ill health," the girl on the inside spoke first, recovering her breath. "I suppose royal persons may lie abed and nurse their dispositions, while poor ones have to keep on washing dishes. But come on into the kitchen, Betty, we are in there to-night and I haven't yet finished my chores."

She led the way with the candle down the shabby hall until both girls entered the lighted room. There, with a little cry of surprise, Betty ran over and dropped down on her knees by the side of a lounge.

The woman on the lounge was not so large as the girl, although her brown hair showed a good deal of gray and her face looked tired and worn. She had been holding a magazine in her hands, but evidently had not been reading, for her eyes had turned from the girl, who stood only a few feet away from her drying some cups and saucers, to the two others who had just come in, without an instant's delay.

"I am quite all right, dear," she answered the

newcomer, "only the kitchen seemed so warm and cozy after the wet day and I was tired."

Betty was too familiar with the lovely, old-fashioned kitchen of her dearest friends even to think about it, but to-night she did look about her for a moment.

The room was the largest in the cottage; the walls were of oak so dark a brown from age that they were almost black; there were heavy rafters across the ceiling and swinging from them bunches of dried, sweet-smelling herbs. The windows had broad sills filled with pots of red geraniums and ground ivy, and as they were wide open the odor of the wet, spring earth outside mingled with the aromatic fragrance of the flowers.

An old stove was set deep into the farthest wall with a Dutch oven at one side and above it a high, severely plain mantel holding a number of venerable pots and pans of pewter and copper and two tall, copper candlesticks. The candles were lighted, as the room was too large for the single light of the lamp on the table near the lounge.

Polly O'Neill had gone straight to her sister and putting both hands on her shoulders had pushed her steadily back inch by inch until she forced her into a large armchair.

"Mollie Mavourneen, you know I hate washing dishes like an owl does the day light, but I am not going to let you do my work and to-night you know the agreeable task of cleaning up belongs to me. I asked you to leave things alone when I went to the door and I don't think you play fair." Polly seized a cup with such vehemence that it slipped from her hand and crashed onto the floor, but neither her mother nor Mollie showed the least sign of surprise and only Betty's eyes widened with understanding.

Strangers always insisted that there were never twin sisters in the world so exactly alike as Mollie and Polly O'Neill (not that their names had ever been intended to rhyme in this absurd fashion, for they had started quite sensibly, as Mary and Pauline), but to the friends who knew them both well this idea was absurd. It was true they were of the same height and their hair and eyes of the same color, their noses and mouths of somewhat the same shape, but with these superficial likenesses the resemblance ended. Anybody should have been able to see that in each detail Polly was the more intense; her hair was blacker and longer, her eyes bluer, her cheek bones a little higher with brighter color and her chin and delicate nose a trifle longer and more pointed. Of the two girls, however, Mollie was the prettier because her features were more regular and her expression more serene; but once under the spell of her sister, one never thought much of her appearance.

Polly had a temperament and she was having an attack of it to-night; the room was fairly electric with it. From some far off Irish ancestor she must have inherited it, for though her father had been an Irishman and had spent forty out of the fifty years of his life in Ireland, he had quite a different disposition and had been as amazed by Polly in her babyhood as the rest of her family.

Captain O'Neill had resigned from the English army eighteen years before and crossed the ocean to spend a few years in the neighborhood of the White Mountains on account of his health; he had no more money than most Irish gentlemen, but had charming manners, was extremely handsome and had soon fallen in love and married a girl twenty years younger than himself. Mary Poindexter had been the girl most loved in Woodford, one of its belles and heiresses, but her money had not amounted to much and soon disappeared after her marriage, until now she had only the cottage in which she and her daughters lived and the income earned by her work as private secretary to Mr. Edward Wharton of "The Wharton Granite Co." Captain O'Neill had lived only until his twin daughters were eight years old and since then the girls and their mother had kept up their small home together.

"You are dead tired and Polly is cross as two sticks and poor Mollie does not know what to do with you. Would you rather I should go away? I only came to tell you something wonderful," Betty whispered in Mrs. O'Neill's ear.

The older woman shook her head. "No, you have come just at the right time. I am not very tired, only my daughters chose to think so and wouldn't let me help with dinner and so, as I am an obedient, well brought-up mother, I am doing as I am told. And Polly is not in a bad humor, at least I hope - "

The girl, who had been picking up the bits of broken china from the kitchen floor, now straightened up and for the first time Betty discovered that she must have been crying a short while before.

"Oh, yes, I am anything you may like to call me," Polly announced indifferently, "and I am not in the least ashamed to have 'The Princess' know it. If Betty had to stand all the things I have stood to-day, she would be in a far worse humor. She and I are not angels like Mary and Mollie, so I suppose that is the reason why we love one another part of the time and hate one another the rest. I am sure I never pretend not to being dreadfully envious of 'The Princess'."

Polly came over and sat down cross-legged on the old rug near her mother and best friend, and though she smiled a little to remove the sting from her words, something in her expression kept Betty from answering at once. In the meantime Mollie joined the group, taking her place at the foot of the lounge.

The three girls were nearly the same age and the closest friends, and Betty probably spent nearly as much of her waking time, at the cottage as she did in her own home, for whenever she was lonely or bored, or, tired perhaps of having too much done for her, she had been used to run across the street to play or work with her friends from the time they were children. Mrs. O'Neill had never seemed very much older than her daughters and had always been called "Mary" by the three girls.

Now Betty reached over and laid one and lightly on Polly. "Don't say we hate no another just because we quarrel now and then and both have bad tempers. I never hate Polly, do I Mary?"

But before Mrs. O'Neill could answer, Polly suddenly faced fiercely about. "I hate you to-night, Betty," she insisted, and then to make her words entirely unlike her actions, slipped one arm around her friend. "Oh, you know that I don't really mean I hate you, I only mean that I am horribly envious and jealous of your having all the money you want and being able to do things without worry, not just things for yourself, but things for other people." And Polly bit her lips and ceased speaking, both because of the note of warning in her mother's face and because the brightness had died away from Betty's.

"I wish you would understand, Polly, that just having things does not necessarily make one happy; I often think it must be nicer to be poor and to have to help like you and Mollie do. This afternoon I was feeling quite forlorn myself, as I had a kind of headache and no one came to see me, and then just like magic from out our haunted chamber there appeared well, I can hardly call her a good fairy, she was too homely, but at least a girl who told me of something so delightful that it sounds almost like a fairy tale. I talked of it to father at dinner and then rushed over to tell you, as I thought you might be interested, but perhaps I had better wait - "

From the foot of the lounge Mollie O'Neill now interrupted. Utterly unlike either her sister or friend in her disposition, her influence often held them together.

"We do want to hear what you have to tell us, Betty, most dreadfully. Just because we happen to be specially worried about something to-night is no reason why Polly should be so mysterious. I vote we tell you what our trouble is and then you tell us your secret."

Polly got up from the floor. She was always curiously intense, not deliberately, but perhaps as a part of her inheritance. Now she made a little bow to Betty. "I am sorry I was rude to you, Princess," she said gently, "but tell you the reason for my special tirade against poverty to-night, I will not and Mollie shall not tell either."

Without replying Betty turned to pick up her blue cloak which had dropped from her shoulders as she knelt by the lounge. It had a cap attached with a blue silk lining and this she slipped over her head.

"It isn't worth while for me to talk of my plan to-night, then," she returned, "for if Polly won't be interested, you and, I could never make a go of it by ourselves, Mollie. Good-night; I promised not to stay very long." Passing by the lounge Mrs. O'Neill reached out, slipping her hand in Betty's and drew her to a place beside her. Usually a girl with the three other girls there was now and then a note in Mrs. O'Neill's voice which they seldom failed to recognize.

"Mollie is right, as Betty is almost one of our family, it is only fair to tell her what has put Polly in her present mood. The truth is, dear, the doctor thinks I am not very well and am needing a rest, so I am being made to lie down every evening after my work, by my daughters, and I am sure when warm weather comes I shall be all right again."

"You won't," Polly interrupted, "and if that is all you mean to tell Betty, why I shall certainly tell her everything now you have started."

Polly went on quickly, with two bright spots of color in her cheeks: "Resting in the evenings is not going to help mother; Dr. Hawkes says she needs months and months of rest and unless she has it she will soon be having a nervous breakdown or something else; that working for nearly eight years in an office supporting herself and two daughters is enough to tire any woman out. Then to-day a wonderful invitation came from my father's relatives, who have never paid the least attention to us before, asking mother to spend the summer with them in Ireland, and - "

Betty's hands were clapped eagerly together as she concluded, "So you are going to accept and Polly's blue at the thought of being separated from you, but really I can't see any reason why I should not have been told of this."

Instead of replying, Polly frowned and Mrs. O'Neill shook her head, so the explanation fell to Mollie. "No, mother is not going to accept; that is what the trouble is and that is why Polly and I sometimes feel cross with you, Betty, because rich people never seem to be able to understand about poor ones. You do what you like without thinking of the money, and we can't do anything we like without thinking of it. Mother feels she can't afford to go."

Looking almost as depressed as her two friends, Betty now turned her back deliberately on both girls to whisper in the older woman's ear.

"Oh, Mary, won't you, can't you; you know how happy it would make us." But she knew her answer even before it was given and also understood that Polly's pride would never have agreed to let her mother accept any favor through her. Indeed, never in all the long years of their friendship had Betty ever dared do half the things she longed to do for her two friends, and indeed Mrs. Ashton often said that Betty accepted far more than she was able to return, since she spent so much of her time in Mrs. O'Neill's home.

"You are awfully foolish, Mary," Betty argued, "because if you should really get ill - "

"That is just what I have been saying, Betty dear, for the past two hours," Polly protested, forgetting the difference between herself and her friend and edging close enough to the lounge to lay her head in, the other girl's lap. "And the worst of it is, Mr. Wharton says mother can have the holiday, he will pay her salary while she is away, and she only won't go because she says she can't leave Mollie and me alone and can't afford to pay any one to look after us. It is so foolish, when we are old enough to be taking care of her! I suppose she wouldn't be afraid to leave Mollie, it is just me! Sometimes it does not seem quite fair to be born a twin, because see how things are put into Mollie divided, all the good got and all the bad into me; so I suppose mother thinks I would set the house on fire or run away and go on the stage as I sometimes threaten, so soon as her back was turned. Oh, Mavourneen darling of the world, the very name of Lake Killarney, where our cousins live, would make you well."

But again Polly stopped talking because Betty had seized her by both shoulders, giving her a decided shake. "Say it again to me quickly. Is it just because Mary does not know what to do with you and Mollie that she won't go away?"

And both sisters nodded silently.

With a cry of what sounded like delight, Betty rose hurriedly to her feet, letting the blue cloak slip away from her for the second time.

Then dancing across the kitchen she seized the two tall

candlesticks from the mantelpiece and setting them down in the center of the floor afterwards added the third, with which Polly had lighted their way through the hall. Above them she made a mystic sign by flattening the fingers of her right hand against those of her left, while slowly she revolved about them chanting: "Wohelo, Wohelo, Wohelo, in you lies the answer to all our difficulties," to the entire amazement of her small audience.

CHAPTER III

"WORK, HEALTH AND LOVE"

"Much learning hath made her mad," sighed Polly mournfully, Betty being a notoriously poor student.

Mollie was staring thoughtfully at their visitor. "That is an Indian folk dance; perhaps Betty is pretending to be Pocahontas," she suggested, with such an evident attempt to explain away her friend's eccentricities that Betty stopped in her dance to laugh, and Polly and Mrs. O'Neill followed suit.

"I am not mad and I am not playing at being Pocahontas, but as usual Mollie is nearer right than her sister Polly because there is a good deal about the Indians in what I want to tell you." Betty sat down before the three shining candles and taking a little stick from the pile of wood near by she pointed it at her third candle. "You are to guess what my strange word, 'Wohelo' means. No, it is not an Indian, word, although it sounds like it. Mary, you begin by taking the last syllable first. What is the greatest thing in the world?"

Mrs. O'Neill, some minutes before, had risen half way up from her lounge and was leaning her head on her arm, while she watched Betty's curious proceedings. "The greatest thing in the world?" she repeated softly.

"Far wiser persons than I found the answer to that question many years ago. The greatest thing in the world is love."

Betty nodded. "Now, Polly, you may have the next guess, though you are sure to say the wrong thing. What is the next greatest thing to love?"

Polly shrugged her thin shoulders, her face still moody in spite of her recently awakened interest. "Oh, I told you the answer to that question when you first came into this room, Betty Ashton, though none of you chose to believe me. It is plain as a pipe-stem to me that wealth is the next best thing to love and sometimes it is better when you happen to love the wrong thing - or person."

"It rhymes with wealth but begins with the letter 'h'," the questioner returned hastily, too much in earnest to waste further time in argument. "Now, Mollie, you have the third turn, remember you are to decide what the first syllable stands for, 'Wo'."

For a few seconds the third girl hesitated, her cheeks flushing uncomfortably. Not so quick or clever with her tongue as Polly and Betty she was far more gifted with her fingers. "I am sure I don't know what you mean," she replied. "'Wo' is the beginning of the word 'woman', but you can't mean woman. I know you and Polly think books of plays and novels the greatest things in the world, but I don't and besides I can't find the right word for them. You know what I really like best is just cooking and cleaning up and putting flowers on the table, stupid household things that can't have anything to do with your wonderful word." And Mollie looked so apologetic for her own domestic tastes that her mother took both her hands and held them tight.

"For goodness' sake, Mollie dear, even in these days of the advanced female it is still something to be proud of, to have real womanly tastes. Because some women go out into the world is no reason why they should lose their womanly instincts. What we are all working for, both men and women, is really just the making of a home, a big or a little one. I don't know myself what word Betty is searching for, but I do believe these very things that you like best come very close to my own guess. For if love is the greatest thing in the world, the making of a home to shelter it is most important. I have an idea that love would come to a tragic end if, when it returned home to dinner, Polly should meet it in the character of Ophelia, with wild flowers in her hair, offering it rosemary and rue for dinner instead of meat and vegetables."

Again the audience laughed because of Polly's well-known devotion to the drama and because if she were left alone to look after the cooking, her mother and Mollie often returned to find her poring over her recitations with the dinner burning on the stove.

"If mother is going to preach a sermon with me for a text, Betty's candles will sputter and die out before ever she explains her word," Polly suggested.

"Oh, the word is 'work'; Mollie wasn't so far wrong, though work may mean different things to different people. Wohelo means 'Work, Health and Love'," Betty explained quickly, still keeping her eyes on the candle flames.

But Polly rising from her place slipped over and took Betty by both shoulders.

"Elizabeth Ashton, more commonly known as 'The Princess,' Bettina or Betty, will you kindly explain yourself? No doubt those are three estimable things you are recommending to us, but please tell me how Work, Health and Love are going to solve our present difficulties and help mother get the rest she needs. It seems to me she has given us too much of the first and last of your watchword already and has too little of the middle thing left in consequence."

Betty's long lashes swept her cheeks in a tantalizing fashion and her color deepened as, clasping her hands over her knees, she began slowly swaying back and forth, her eyes fastened on Polly.

"I am dreadfully long in coming to my point," she confessed, "but it is such fun to keep you guessing and I do so want you to be interested. You see, I suppose you know about the Camp Fire Girls, everybody seems to have heard except me, but now 'That light which has been given to me, I desire to pass undimmed to others.' Will you, won't you, will you, won't you be a Camp Fire Girl?" Her manner, which had been a queer combination of fun and seriousness, now at last appeared entirely grave. "Mollie and Polly," she continued quietly, "You know how often we have talked lately of being dissatisfied, of feeling that here we are growing older and older every day and yet not learning half the things we ought to learn nor having half the fun we ought to have. Of course we read novels all the time, because it is the only way for nice girls to learn about romance or adventure, but we would like really to live the things we think about just the same as boys do. They don't dream and scold about the things they want to do; they go ahead and do them, teaching one another by working things out together. They belong to things and don't just have to have things belong to them' to make them happy like girls do."

"Hear, hear!" cried Polly, not exactly seeing what Betty was driving at and desiring to tease her into greater confusion.

But as Mrs. O'Neill shook her head encouragingly, Betty would not deign to consider her tormentor.

"Oh, it is foolish for me to try to explain all the Camp Fire idea means," she added simply. "I couldn't if I tried, for Esther Clark, the strange girl who has been living at the asylum and has just come to our house, only told me what she knew this afternoon. But I want to find out by living the Camp Fire idea, I want to see what we could get out of forming a Camp Fire Club, the first one here in Woodford. Just take Polly and Mollie and me, for example, Mary dear," she continued coaxingly. "I am longing to know the things Mollie does about cooking and housekeeping and all the rest and I can't learn at home. Think what it means to go messing about in our kitchen with, cook and half a dozen servants laughing at you! Then Mollie really would like to know what Polly and I find so fascinating in books and in prowling about together in the woods and Polly - well, I don't know that she wishes to learn anything from Mollie or me or anybody else who joins our club, but if she doesn't, that is just what she ought to learn."

Polly held up both hands. "For goodness sake, Betty,

stop talking, I will join your Camp Fire Club and be made an example of at any time, also I will use my noble influence to persuade any girls you wish to join. All the same I don't see what your wretched club has to do with helping us solve our problem about mother, and that is all I care about at present."

"Has to do, - why everything," Betty repeated slowly. But before she was able to finish her sentence there was a sudden loud ringing of the front door bell and the three girls jumped to their feet. In another moment Polly had disappeared into the hall, returning with her expression changed again to its original look of gloom.

"It's that granite man, mother, Mr. Wharton, with his entire family, son and daughter. I wonder why they can't leave you alone after business hours? I had to ask them in the parlor, since we can't entertain any one in the kitchen except 'The Princess,' but we simply can't join you until we hear what she has to say."

Polly sighed as her mother rose without replying and left the room, and Betty did he her best to hide her smiles, for everybody in Woodford believed that Mrs. O'Neill's employer had more than a friendly interest in her, and though Polly constantly railed at their poverty and Mr. Wharton was the richest man in the village, the very sound of his name used often to irritate her.

The candles had at last burned down to their sockets and softly Betty blew out the last flickering flames. With a nod of understanding Mollie turned down the lighted lamp and after a fashion of many years the three girls drew three little old fashioned rockers in a semicircle up before the kitchen fire.

"My plan is to form our Camp Fire Club of just the right girls and to have just the right guardian and then to spend our whole summer camping in the woods," Betty explained quickly at last. "You see I don't want to go to Europe with mother and father this summer one bit, I am dead tired of hotels and sights. So at dinner to-night I talked over the Camp Fire plan with father and though mother wasn't enthusiastic I could see father didn't think it in the least a bad idea, so I am sure he will give us the camping outfit if I beg very hard and we can all share expenses afterwards. Can't you understand that if Mary lets you spend your summer in camp she can go away and rest and think no more about you and we can have such a wonderful time."

In the half darkness Polly danced a shadow dance and then flung her arms about her friend. "Oh, Princess, I might have known you were as clever as 'Sentimental Tommy' and would surely 'find a wa'. I am sure mother will think it a beautiful plan for us. Just to live among the trees and the stars and hear the birds sing, and tell stories about our own camp fire and to sing."

"Yes, and to do our own cooking and cleaning and wood gathering and a thousand other practical things," laughed Betty, to stop Polly's rhapsodizing. "But the truly important part of our scheme is to find congenial girls for our club and the right guardian."

"There are four of us already," Mollie suggested.

Betty appeared surprised. "Just you and Polly and me; what fourth girl do you mean?"

As Mollie did not answer at once, a low whistle came

from between Polly's closed lips. "Do you mean, Princess, that you do not intend to invite the girl who told you about the Camp Fire Club, Esther Clark? I know her by sight at school."

Betty frowned. "Certainly I had not meant to include her; she does not belong to our set. I don't mean to be rude, but she has been raised in an orphan asylum and nobody knows who she is. I suppose she comes of some very common family."

"Common families sometimes produce very uncommon characters," Polly returned dryly. "And s-n-o-b spells snob, but not Betty, I hope. I wish you wouldn't think so much about 'family', Princess; I do believe we ought to judge people by what they are themselves and not by what their ancestors have been."

With a quick movement Betty half overturned her chair. "Good-night," she said, "we can talk things over to-morrow. I promised not to be too late to-night. It isn't that I really mind having Esther in our club, only we don't know her very well and it seems most important that we should all be congenial."

But Betty could not move toward the door because her skirts were held fast. "If you go now I shall cry my eyes out all night," Polly protested in a tone that was almost convincing. "It was horrid of me, darling, to tell you the truth and me Irish and believin' in the blarney stone," she apologized in her Pollyesque fashion. "Please never, never tell me the truth about myself and have anybody in your club you like. Only if you expect to have twelve girls who exactly agree you will have to leave both you and me out to start with."

Betty laughed, only half appeased, but Mollie was speaking quietly and because she talked less frequently than the other two girls they usually paused to listen to her.

"I think the more unlike we girls are the more fun we will have and the more we will help one another," she suggested. "But, Betty, do you know who has started this Camp Fire idea in Woodford and who knows just what we ought to do?"

Betty groaned. "Who else could it be, my dear, but my arch-enemy, the person I like least and who likes me even less in all this village. Ah, is anything ever perfect in this life? Martha McMurtry, the science teacher at the high school, who will certainly cause me to remain in the sophomore class another year unless I learn something more than what H20 means, is the only woman Esther could suggest."

The sisters laughed, since Betty's battles with this teacher had kept things lively.

"You poor dear, we can't have her for our guardian," Polly insisted sympathetically. "Can you imagine such a prim, scientific old maid ever understanding anything of the beauty and romance of life in the woods? I would like Titania, Queen of the Fairies, to be our only chaperon."

Before the other girls could dispute the absurdity of Polly's final suggestion, the kitchen door opened and Mrs. O'Neill returned looking unusually cross. "Why didn't you join me, you wicked children?" she said reproachfully. "Mr. Wharton came to ask me, since I was not going away, to look after his little girl this summer. He has to leave on some business trip and as Frank is to camp in the woods, there was nothing for the poor man to do with Sylvia. I hope you won't mind very much, for I have promised to take care of her."

"Sylvia!" The three voices made a dismal chorus.

"That stupid, ill-mannered child! I am sorry, dear, but you are not going to look after anything or anybody this summer but yourself. You see you are sailing for Ireland in a few weeks and we are going to live in the woods and be taken care of by our old mother earth and our father, the sun," Polly replied dramatically.

"You are talking nonsense, Polly; please don't be tiresome any more to-night," Mrs. O'Neill urged, lying down on the sofa again, as though she were too weary to be up another minute. "I can't discuss the matter with you, but Mr. Wharton has been too kind for me to refuse him this request."

Betty found her blue cloak again and softly slipped over to kiss the older woman good-night. "Don't worry, what Polly told you is true, but Sylvia shall be looked after just the same."

She slipped away, Polly following to watch her safely across the street as she always did. Outdoors the girls stood silent for a moment looking up at the beauty of the night. The stars were shining and the warmth the day had failed to bring to the earth had been followed by some unseen messenger of the night.

"You are going to include that hateful child in your Camp Fire Club after what I said to you, Betty?" Polly whispered. "Oh, if only her name wasn't Sylvia and she didn't have a snub nose and wear goggles I could forgive her. But think how absurd the combination is! Anyhow you are a dear, and it must be because I am Irish that I am always in the wrong."

CHAPTER IV

"MEG"

Thump, thump, thump came the sound of a heavy object rolling slowly step by step down a long stairway and then after an interval of ten seconds a prolonged, ear-piercing roar.

Immediately a girl darted out of a room on the second floor of a pretty brick house, colliding with a young man several years older, who came forth at the same time from his own room across the hall.

"Great Scott, Meg, what are you doing only half-dressed at this hour of the day?" he demanded with brotherly contempt.

"We will discuss my costume or lack of it later," she returned, holding her short flannel dressing sacque together and laughing over her shoulder where one long blond plait hung neatly braided, the rest of her hair falling loose. "Methinks that was Horace Virgil Everett trying to break up the furniture somewhere! Was there ever such an infant born into this suffering world? I simply never turn my back without his getting into fresh trouble."

While she was talking she was also running

Margaret Vandercook

downstairs, followed in a more leisurely manner by her brother. Both of them glanced into the empty library and untidy dining-room as they passed and finally arrived in a dark passageway at the end of the back stairs.

A small object lay on the floor with its arms and legs outspread, showing not the slightest inclination to pick itself up, and on Meg's bending over it the wails broke out afresh.

"Oh, do shut up, 'Bumps'," Jack Everett said good-naturedly. "You haven't killed yourself and you're much too big for Meg to carry."

But the small boy clung desperately to his sister, his fat arms about her neck and his legs about her waist until with difficulty she was able to get him upstairs and into her own room.

He was probably about three feet high and almost as broad, between three and four years old, with brown hair that would stand up in a pompadour simply because it was too stiff to lie down, a perfectly insignificant nose, a Cupid's bow of a mouth and two large grave blue eyes, as innocent of mischief as any lamb's.

At the present moment, however, his eyes were simply raining tears, as though they had their source in a cloudburst, and over one of them a bump appeared as large as an egg. Indeed, Horace Virgil, named for his Professor father's favorite Latin poets, had been rechristened 'Bumps' by his older brother and was more commonly known by that title.

Meg kept glancing at the clock as she dampened her small brother's forehead with witch hazel. "I am afraid I can't go," she said in a disappointed tone, "and I am dreadfully sorry because I promised. But if I leave Horace with the servants now he will howl himself ill. I don't suppose you were going to stay in for a few hours. Oh, of course not!" she concluded, seeing that her older brother was wearing his khaki service uniform and held a big, broad-brimmed hat in his hand. "Heigh-ho, don't I wish I were a boy," she sighed whimsically, turning at last toward her mirror, decorated with college flags, and beginning to braid the second half of her hair.

John Everett, frowned and fidgeted. "I am sorry, Meg," he replied after a moment. "I would stay at home, only there is a meeting of my brigade and when a fellow belongs to a thing why he owes it some of his time. I don't see why you have to stay at home so much. Of course it is a good deal for a girl to have to look after, a house and father and the kid and me, but you have two maids and if you only were a better manager. Why you don't seem even to take time to dress like other girls, you are always kind of flying apart with a button off your waist or the braid torn on your skirt, and I do love a spick and span girl. Why don't you look like Betty Ashton, she's always up to the limit?"

Margaret Everett coiled her yellow plaits about her head, keeping her back turned to hide the trembling of her lips until she was able to answer cheerfully. "Why yes, I should like to look like 'The Princess' and wear clothes like she does, but in the first place I am not so good looking as Betty, I haven't a maid to see after my clothes and fifty dollars a month to dress on - and I haven't a mother."

Margaret Vandercook

Jack Everett flushed. He was a splendid looking fellow, big and brown, with light hair of almost the same coppery tones as his sister's, and although but eighteen was nearly six feet tall. It was his last year at the Male High School of which his father was President, and already he had passed with high honors his entrance examinations for Dartmouth College.

"Oh, I say. Meg, don't pile it on," he protested. "You are handsome enough all right, and it was only on your own account that I was wishing you could run things better."

Meg had evidently given up the idea of her engagement by this time, for she had seated herself in a big chair with her small brother on her lap and was rocking him slowly back and forth, his head resting on her shoulder.

"You are right, Jack, I am not offended," she answered. "I know I am a poor manager, but somehow I don't just take to housekeeping and mothering naturally. Men always think girls know such things by instinct. They don't understand that we have to learn them just as boys learn bookkeeping or office work and I have never had any one to teach me."

"The late Miss Everett," a new voice called unexpectedly, apparently coming from about midway up the front steps. "Meg, may I come on upstairs, the front door was half open and I knew full well that you would never keep your promise to me unless I came and got you."

Meg put down her small burden hastily and John unconsciously stiffened his broad shoulders until his appearance was more than ever military.

"Come on up, Betty dear, I am sorry I am such a sight, but the baby has just gotten hurt and I have to give up the club meeting," Meg called back.

The next instant Betty Ashton appeared at the open bedroom door, wearing a light woolen motor coat, a blue hat with a red-brown wing in it fitting close over her hair which was tucked up out of sight in a very grown-up fashion. She had a great deal of color and her eyes were bright with desire.

"Oh, you can't disappoint me, Meg; I shall never forgive you," she protested, and then came to a sudden stop seeing that John Everett was also in her friend's room. But as he bowed low to her it was impossible for him to have observed her slight blush.

"Do take Meg with you by force, Miss Ashton," he urged. (It was always quite thrilling to Betty at fifteen to be called "Miss Ashton," and no other boy of her acquaintance seemed to realize that one could grow out of being addressed as "Betty".) "She spoils the small boy and all the rest of us far too much. 'Bumps' has just taken another tumble." Jack Everett then backed out of the room in soldierly fashion and at the instant of his disappearance Betty tucked her arms about the small Horace, critically surveying his injured eye.

"Do hurry and get dressed, Meg, that's a dear. You know we simply can't get on without you this afternoon. I will button you up in a jiffy and we can take this bumptious little person along with us. He will probably escape and fall down somewhere while we are having our meeting, but we can both keep our eyes on him."

"He would be too much trouble," Meg demurred, but already she was surveying her only clean shirt waists, a blue and a white one, to see which was in the better state of repair. The blue was faded but whole, so she slipped into it, letting Betty button it up the back, and then with her brother's words still rankling in her mind carefully adjusted her skirt at, the belt. "You are awfully good to let me come this afternoon, Betty, because I told you it would be just impossible for me to spend the summer with you girls as it would be for me to take a trip to the moon. John is going camping and father is to have a summer lecture course in Boston and - "

"Oh yes, and you are to stay at home and take care of this house and baby! I don't think it is fair, or that your father or brother in the least realize what you do for them. But see here, dear, if what I thinks is true, as my old nurse used to say, and you come to be a Camp Fire girl this summer, why you will learn an awful lot about keeping house and being first aid to broken babies and everything you need to know. Never mind, don't let's argue about the question now, just come along, for the motor is waiting at the gate. Nearly all the girls I have asked must be at home by this time, but I have to collect two more people, Martha McMurtry - you know how I love her - and yet she carries the information in her brain of the right way to organize a Camp Fire club. Also there is Eleanor Meade; being a genius, you know Eleanor can't be expected to remember anything, should a wave of inspiration happen to flow over her."

CHAPTER V

THEIR FIRST MEETING

The drawing-room at the Ashton homestead ran the whole length of one side of the house and on this particular May afternoon was so filled with sunshine and light that even the old portraits on the walls appeared to change their severe Puritanical expressions and to look down, from out their heavy gold frames, with something almost approaching friendliness, on the strange girl now alone in the room, although nothing in her appearance or manner suggested the birth and breeding partly responsible for their New England pride.

The girl was also humbly engaged in placing fresh flowers on the tables and mantel and in rearranging the chairs and ornaments in the room to their best advantage. Finally, after a lingering glance out the front window, she picked up her last vase of flowers, a single branch of apple blossoms in a tall, green jar, and, crossing over to the grand piano so placed it that the sunlight shone full upon it. Then she stood for a moment looking thoughtfully at the open keyboard, which had a small sheet of music spread before it. Esther Clark next sat down at the piano and lightly ran her fingers over the keys so that it could scarcely have been possible for any one farther away than the

Margaret Vandercook

adjoining hall to have heard her playing. The refrain was simple and repeated itself, yet had dramatic force and lingered in one's memory, the musical call of the watchword for the Camp Fire Girls.

Only that morning Betty had asked Esther to try to teach this call to her friends when they came together at her home that afternoon to form their club, and though Esther was painfully shy she felt obliged to do her best. Some few of Betty's friends were known to her through their acquaintance at school, but into not one of their homes had she ever been invited socially.

The door of the drawing-room farthest from the piano opened quietly.

"Betty," a young man's voice inquired reproachfully, "aren't you even glad enough to see me to say hello? When before did I ever know you so devoted to practicing that you wouldn't stop for any excuse, and yet here I have come all the way home from Portsmouth on your account!"

Richard Ashton ceased talking abruptly, for instead of the pretty figure of his sister, Betty, he now beheld rising from the piano stool a tall girl with bright red hair, looking as though she had been frightened speechless.

"Great Caesar's ghost, what a homely girl!" was his first thought, but not a change in his expression revealed what was in the young man's mind as he stretched forth his hand.

"I am sorry to have interrupted you," he said quickly, "but I am Richard Ashton, Betty's brother."

Of course he expected that the strange girl would then answer him, at least tell him who she was or give some explanation of her presence, but instead Esther stood silently looking down at the floor and twisting her hands together in a wholly unnecessary state of embarrassment.

Richard Ashton was of medium height, slenderly built, but with broad shoulders, and at this time of life twenty-three years old. His hair and eyes were light brown; he bore no resemblance to Betty and had a curiously serious expression for so young and fortunate a fellow. Although not handsome, Dick had a look of purpose and distinction and always had unconsciously served as the ideal for Betty's girl friends. He was a Princeton graduate, but was now studying medicine in Portsmouth and expected later to continue his studies in Germany. Perhaps it was his own seriousness and settled purpose that had made him assist in spoiling his small sister almost from her babyhood, yet lately seeing Betty's restlessness and discontent he had begun to wonder if he and his father and mother had been as kind to her as they had meant to be. Betty was growing up and it might be she too needed to have something asked of her, that she too wished to give as well as to receive.

"I am not your sister's friend (the girl near the piano had finally made up her mind to speak), I am only a kind of companion, to help her with her studying or to do whatever she desires."

Dick Ashton laughed, his face immediately losing its look of gravity. "Well, that is no particular reason why you should not be her friend as well, is it? At least I hope Betty won't make the task too hard for you, but as to doing all the things she desires, I am afraid that will keep you pretty busy. I believe I remember now, my mother did write me about asking you to come here to stay; you have lived before - " The young man hesitated. But Esther had now come nearer and really she seemed almost too plain even to serve his pretty sister, Betty, the contrast might be too hard for the homely girl.

"You were playing something when I came in, won't you go on," Dick continued hastily, fearing that the strange girl, with her pale eyes fixed on his, might be able to read his inmost thoughts and not desiring to hurt her feelings. However she had started, edging toward the door. "I would much rather not; your sister is to have some friends here this afternoon and wishes me to teach them a few lines of music. I hope your mother won't mind my touching this splendid piano."

"What on earth is the girl afraid of? I have no desire to eat her," Richard thought to himself, continuing to observe Esther's frightened expression and nervous manner, but only answering good-naturedly: "Certainly she won't mind. Please use the piano whenever you like, for Betty hates practicing and I don't care much for a man musician, especially a poor one, though I love music."

Just for a moment the newcomer's timidity vanished and her smile of pleasure, showing her big, strong mouth with its white teeth, relieved her face of its entire plainness. "I should love it more than anything in the world; would you mind asking your mother if I may? I am afraid to ask her."

"But not afraid of asking me?" Richard laughed; he

had made his suggestion without any special thought, but the girl might as well be allowed to bang at their piano if she liked. Should she get it out of order why it could soon be straightened out again. And then kindness to persons less fortunate than himself was second nature with Richard Ashton.

"Here is the mater coming, I will ask her at once," he returned, and then seeing Esther's unspoken look of entreaty, as he went forward to open the door for his mother, he silently agreed to post one his request.

Mrs. Ashton was a tall, blonde, handsomely dressed woman, who rarely showed affection for anyone save her husband and children and whose leisure time was largely devoted to playing bridge. Neither Betty nor her son looked like her. Richard resembled his father, while Betty must have inherited her appearance from some more remote ancestor. In one comer of the parlor hung an oil painting of one of Mr. Ashton's great-aunts, a young English girl in a white muslin dress and picture hat, whom Betty always insisted she resembled.

Mrs. Ashton was frowning anxiously.

"Hasn't Betty returned, Dick?" she inquired. "It is an hour since luncheon and her friends may arrive at any moment. The child was not at all well yesterday and, I do wonder if her science teacher can be keeping her in, Miss McMurtry is so inconsiderate. I really don't know what to do about Betty this summer, she is so opposed to going to Europe with us again and wants to form a club or a camp, something perfectly extraordinary, so as to spend her summer in the woods. She almost talked your father into the idea last evening, but I do hope, dear Richard, that you will oppose her. You have such influence with Betty."

Dick and his mother were standing together by the window now on the lookout, for the truant. "Don't be such a weakling, mother," the young man replied teasingly. "If you really wish Betty to go to Europe with you and father say so and let that settle the matter, but I am not so sure this new scheme of hers is a bad one. Betty sent me a night telegram at bedtime last night (telephoned it, I suppose, when you thought she was in bed) asking me to come home for the day and help her get her own way. Living out of doors all summer, mother, and learning to look after herself and to rub up against other girls may be the best thing in the world for Betty. I am afraid she has been growing up to be more ornamental than useful."

"There is no reason why Betty should be anything but ornamental," Mrs. Ashton argued, although plainly thinking over her son's words.

Dick Ashton shook his head. "No, mother, the modern world has no place in it but for useful people nowadays. And somehow it seems to me that even more is going to be asked of women than has been asked of men. They have got to do their own housekeeping and some of the world's too, pretty soon."

Before the young fellow finished speaking he and his mother were both smiling and waving their hands toward Mollie and Polly O'Neill, who were at this moment crossing the street with several other girl friends. Before they entered the house, however, Betty's automobile, driven by herself, dashed into sight, containing five other passengers: Margaret

Everett and her small brother; Miss McMurtry, the science teacher at the high school; a tall girl with a clever face and a far-away expression in her near-sighted blue eyes; and a fifth girl, an entire stranger both to Mrs. Ashton and Dick and until a short while before an equal stranger to Betty.

Almost before the car stopped Betty was out of her seat and ushering her visitors into their big, sweet-smelling drawing-room. There Esther stood close against the wall, trying her best to shrink out of sight even while she reproached herself for her unnecessary awkwardness and fear. Suppose she had had no home and no social training like the greater number of these other girls, yet did she not mean to follow forever the law of the Camp Fire and would it not teach her in time to gain the knowledge necessary to happiness?

CHAPTER VI

THE LAW OF THE CAMP FIRE

"Esther, won't you repeat the Law of the Camp Fire for the girls?" Miss McMurtry asked, fifteen minutes later, when Betty's guests were seated in a close circle about the drawing-room, their faces eager with curiosity.

Esther alone sat at some distance from the others, so that Betty was compelled to draw her forward toward the center of their group. How she longed to refuse to recite, for instead of a dozen pairs of eyes fastened upon her she felt there must be at least a hundred! Yet catching an expression of amused sympathy on Dick Ashton's face somehow she felt encouraged to go on.

"Esther and I have been studying the plan of the Camp Fire organization for the past two months and it is really very simple," Miss McMurtry continued. "One must just follow certain general rules and then add whatever seems appropriate to give one's special camp originality and character. I had been hoping to form a club in the village this summer, but of course if we can carry out Betty's idea and spend our summer together in the woods, why we will learn in a few months what it might have taken us years to find out in weekly meetings in town." The young woman stopped, turning toward Esther, and the girl then felt obliged to speak.

Esther's voice was low, but had that rare quality given to but a few voices of being heard at even a great distance without being raised.

"Seek beauty. Give service. Pursue knowledge. Be trustworthy. Hold on to health. Glorify work. Be happy."

With each line, feeling the sympathy of her small audience increase, Esther gained courage until at last she was able to finish her verse with fervor and conviction.

After her conclusion most of the faces near her were unusually thoughtful until Polly O'Neill, seated next Mrs. Ashton, gave a characteristic laugh followed by a sigh.

"My dear children, if we ever learn to live up to that law of the Camp Fire, then shall we be angels and not girls!" she exclaimed.

And she might have added more had not an imploring frown from Betty silenced her. Of course some of the girls would understand that Polly rarely meant what she said, but there we're other members of the little company with whom Betty wished to take no risks. Besides, Polly's laugh could sometimes dampen even her own enthusiasm! And had she not placed her friend next her mother in order that she might interest Mrs. Ashton in their plan, for Polly was a great favorite with the older woman and never afraid of using her pretty blarney stone with her.

However, except for a laugh no one seemed in the least influenced by Polly's skepticism.

"We can at least try to live up to the law," Mollie replied quietly, answering from her chair a few feet away.

In a few moments, however, Betty no longer feared the effect of her friend's attitude. Perhaps to some of the girls the idea of a summer camp seemed too beautiful to be possible, yet plainly the ideals of the Camp Fire organization, as Miss McMurtry explained them more fully, had fired their imaginations, filling them with new hopes and enthusiasm.

Meg had been listening to what had been said with glowing cheeks, meaning to become a Camp Fire girl even though it was entirely impossible for her to join the summer camp. She was holding her small brother tight in her arms, trying to distract his attention with objects to be seen out the front window, and so entirely oblivious of the fact that the hastily adjusted hairpins had been slipping out of her hair, until one yellow braid now dangled over her pink ear.

Mollie O'Neill's cheeks were also flushed, but she sat perfectly still, keeping her hands clasped tight together in a fashion she had when desiring a thing greatly and not feeling sure she would receive it.

Eleanor Meade had even forgiven Betty for dragging her away from her unfinished painting of the May, sky (a painting which Meg and Betty had assured her resembled soap suds), so enthralled had she become with the summer plan. If her parents could be persuaded to allow her to stay in camp with the girls during the summer, why then surely she need not be bothered with having to take exercise and help with the housework, as her mother insisted, she could simply give up all her time to her drawing and painting. You see Eleanor, like a good many other girls, did not at once grasp the meaning of the Camp Fire idea.

Apparently only one person in Mrs. Ashton's drawing-room up to this time seemed to have gotten nothing at all out of Miss McMurtry's explanations and the girls' discussion of a Camp Fire club. But then how could she, for Sylvia Wharton apparently had not listened and certainly had never taken her eyes from Polly's face? She appeared a stupid child, short and stout and, although fourteen, hardly seemed more than twelve. Her clothes were expensive but always inappropriate, indeed they were far too handsome for such a plain little girl. However, they were in accord with her father's taste, and although Mr. Wharton was now a wealthy man, he had begun life as a stone-cutter and could hardly be expected to know much about the proper way to dress a small, motherless daughter.

Several times in the past half hour Polly had almost yielded to the inclination to implore Sylvia to take her eyes off her, for the little girl did not look sensitive and her eyes were so large and expressionless they made one uncomfortable, but then Polly forbore, until, as her own interest in their meeting proceeded, she forgot all about her inquisitor.

It must have been about five o'clock when Betty at last arose and holding a curiously wrought silver ring, a bracelet and a pin in her hand, started to walk slowly about among the circle of her guests.

"If you wish to join our Camp Fire club this afternoon," she invited coaxingly, "you are simply to repeat the lines Esther has just recited for us. Then

Miss McMurtry says you may each receive a woodgatherers' ring. Afterwards, when we have acquired sufficient honors in the seven crafts, 'Health Craft, Home Craft, Nature Lore, Camp Craft, Business and Patriotism'," (Betty repeated the list slowly as though not quite certain of herself), "why then we may attain next to the rank of Fire-Makers and wear their bracelets. The highest honor of all, which I for one shall probably never attain, is to become a Torch Bearer and receive the Torch Bearer's pin. It is all right for me to give the girls the rings, isn't it, Miss McMurtry, after they have repeated the law to you?" Betty asked, "since you have been appointed official guardian by the headquarters in New York? Later on I suppose the girls will tell us when they will wish to come into camp."

Miss McMurtry laughed. Never until this afternoon had she had any liking for Betty Ashton. They were such utterly different types of woman and girl! Yet, now Betty s habit of expecting to have her own way, which her teacher so disliked, was assuredly making their Camp Fire plans go ahead with a rush.

"Yes, I am a properly appointed guardian," Miss McMurtry answered slowly, "and Esther and I have been studying the Camp Fire program until she is almost ready to become a Fire-Maker, but I wonder if, you girls wish me to be your guardian in camp this summer? Perhaps I am not suited to it!" She turned to look at Betty, but failing to catch her eye, looked toward Polly. For the same reason both girls kept their heads bowed, until Betty was finally able to reply with as much enthusiasm as she could muster:

"Oh, of course we wish you, and we shall try to give as

little trouble as possible." Really in her present enthusiasm Betty believed that she and her science teacher would be able to put away all past differences and live in perfect accord under the influence of their new ideals.

Miss McMurtry now turned again to Esther; there were special reasons for her unusual interest in this girl, although even Esther herself was unaware of them.

"You are wearing your bead chains, aren't you?" the new guardian asked, slipping two narrow strips of leather, one strung with orange and the other with bright red beads, from about Esther's throat. "You see each one of these beads represents some honor a girl has attained in the Camp Fire," she explained, "so the girl who finally arrives at the rank of Torch Bearer, really an assistant to the guardian, may own seven different chains of bead, one color for each of the seven crafts."

"My honors so far have been won in health and home craft because of what I was taught at the orphan asylum," Esther added frankly and then blushed uncomfortably, for several of Betty's friends were staring at her curiously. What had inspired Mrs. Ashton and Betty, supposed to be the most exclusive persons in Woodford, to introduce this unknown girl into their home as though she were a member of their family?

Moreover, Betty must have suffered another change of heart for she was now engaged in almost forcing a Wood-Gatherer's ring upon the stranger whom she had lately brought home in the automobile with her.

Mrs. Ashton lifted her lorgnettes to gaze at the visitor. "Tell me, Polly dear," she whispered, "who is that girl with whom Betty is now talking? She is not one of her school friends and yet I feel I have seen her somewhere before, though I am not able to place her."

Polly smiled, shaking her head. "You have seen her, I know I have many times, although she is not a friend or even an acquaintance of mine. But I don't know what has happened to 'The Princess', so I would rather you would put your question to her after we go away."

Mrs. Ashton kept hold of Polly's hand. Two maids had just come into the drawing-room at this moment and were passing plates of cake and cups of hot chocolate about among the guests. The greater number of the girls were crowding around Miss McMurtry and Betty, so only Dick Ashton happened to notice that no one, not even a maid, had come near Esther. Securing chocolate and cake for her himself, he sat down next her, talking but asking no questions, since he feared to embarrass her as he had earlier in the afternoon.

"Do you think, Polly, that this is really a good plan of Betty's?" Mrs. Ashton inquired thoughtfully. "She has seemed so restless and dissatisfied lately. Of course I don't understand all this Camp Fire idea seems to mean to her, I suppose I would have to be a girl again to understand thoroughly, but there may be possibilities in it. Even a conventional society woman longs sometimes to get away from her monotonous life, and surely you will find romance and adventure awaiting you in the woods. I have decided I shall not stand in Betty's way, I shall go away this summer and leave you girls to work things out together, then when I return I may be able to discover what miracles have been wrought in you."

"Oh, you will find us entirely reformed," Polly answered carelessly, not realizing that she of all the girls in the room would be the one to bear the ordeal of fire, the symbol that cleanses and purifies.

But both the girl and woman suddenly became silent, for Dick Ashton had persuaded Esther Clark to the piano and now the entire group of guests closed in about her.

Once again she was singing the morning and evening hymn of the Camp Fire Girls' "My Soul's Desire."

Mrs. Ashton sat listening intently with an odd expression of something almost like relief crossing her face. "Polly dear," she whispered unexpectedly at the close of Esther's song, "perhaps life does even things up more justly than we know, for this strange girl, Esther Clark, has a truly remarkable voice."

CHAPTER VII

WHITE CLOUDS

"White clouds, whose shadows haunt the deep, Light mists, whose soft embraces keep The sunshine on the bills asleep."

The sun was just rising above the crests of a group of the White Mountains called long ago by the indians "Waumbek" because of their snowy foreheads. But this morning, instead of shining like crystal, the snow at their summits was opal tinted rose, yellow and violet from the early rays of the June sun.

Sunrise Hill, standing in the foreground, seemed to catch an even stronger reflection from the sky, for the colors drained down its sides until they emptied into a small, wooded lake at its base.

On either side this hill the sloping lands were a soft green and the meadows beyond golden with the new summer grain, but only fifty yards away a grove of pine trees made a deep mass of shade, and with the birds in their branches singing their daily matins, suggested an old cathedral choir.

The singers were evidently indifferent to intruders, for, close by, four white tents were pitched in a square as though a caravan had halted on its travels. But the caravaneers must have been in the place for some days and showed no intention of moving on, for their arrangements had been made with the idea of permanent comfort.

Around each tent a narrow trench several inches deep had been dug to prevent flooding in case of rain, farther off two large bins held all rubbish until such time as it could be conveniently burned. The camp ground was also beautifully clean, not a scrap of paper nor a tin can could be seen anywhere, and even the grass itself had been swept with a novel, but at the same time, a very old-fashioned broom, for a stake tightly bound with a few sprigs of birch rested against one of the tents, plainly - from the evidences about it - the kitchen tent. At a safe distance a camp fire was smoldering, a fire built according to the best scout methods. Two stout stakes driven slantwise in the ground with three logs cut the same length, one on top the other, resting against these stakes. On either side this elevation two logs lay on the ground like fire logs, with a third crossing them in front, and inside this enclosure a bed of ashes still glowed, carefully covered over for the night. On the lake two birch bark canoes were moored to willow stakes, and hanging on a line stretching from a tree to a pole a number of girls' bathing suits flapped and danced in the air, but no human being was yet in sight.

Suddenly there came a ripple of music from one of the pine trees, "Whee-you, whee-you," a small bird with a spotted breast and a cream-buff coat sang to itself and then began a whistling, ringing monotone that for a moment silenced the other bird chorus.

A girl in a dark red dressing gown quietly opened a tent flap.

"There, the morning has come at last, for that is the voice of 'Oopehanka', the thrush. So after a week in the woods I really am beginning to recognize some of the birds and the Indian names for them." She clapped her hands softly together.

"Oh, Princess, do wake up and let us have a swim before any one else wakens," she whispered imploringly.

Then disappearing inside her tent, she knelt by a bed of hemlock branches covered with soft blue blankets. "Princess," she whispered again.

A sleepy voice answered. "Polly child, please go back to bed, it must be the middle of the night and I ache all over from carrying water and digging trenches. Who could have supposed camping would be such a lot of work!"

"Or such a lot of joy!" Polly laughed. "Ah, Betty, I thought you were yearning to be useful; think of the honor beads you mean to earn! But come now and be useful to me; do let us have a swim together."

Betty was never proof against her friend's pleading. "All right," she agreed, searching about near her bed for her sandals while Polly wrapped a light woolen gown about her, "I don't know whether Miss McMurtry will like our going off by ourselves, but I don't remember her having said we should not, though Camp Fire life does mean doing things together."

The two girls had been talking in the lowest possible tones and were now tiptoeing softly out of their tent, when another voice from another bed interrupted them.

"Betty and Polly, you are sneaks!" Mollie O'Neill exclaimed indignantly. "Just because I can't swim as well as you do and Esther can't swim at all, you are going off without us. You are fine Camp Fire girls; please bring our bathing suits here, too."

Both girls nodded and laughed in rather an abashed fashion. But at a safe distance away Betty turned to Polly. "Won't you confess, please, that it is rather a nuisance having Esther Clark in the tent with us? I don't see why Martha McMurtry insisted upon it when we might have had Meg or most anybody else."

Polly looked unusually grave. "You don't care for Esther, do you?" she questioned. "It is curious, because though you haven't been particularly nice to her, she is devoted to you and I believe would do anything in the world for you."

Ten minutes later the four girls in their Camp Fire bathing suits were in the waters of the lake near their camp, Polly and Betty swimming with long even strokes toward its center, Mollie hovering near the shore, while Esther stood shivering in a foot of water trying vainly to warm herself by splashing and throwing handfuls of water on her chest and face.

Half a mile out Betty turned over on her side. "Say the Law of the Camp Fire to yourself, Polly. I have just said it and I am going back toward shore. I suppose if one makes a vow to 'give service' it is little enough to show another girl how to swim. If Esther didn't look so big and wasn't so horribly shy, I am sure I should like her better, but here goes!"

It wasn't easy work teaching Esther to swim, for she was so much larger than Betty and had such an absurd fashion of keeping both feet down and splashing the water into her own and her teacher's face. Polly laughed softly to herself as she swam slowly forward to offer her assistance. She was wondering if a single week in camp had really begun to reform her spoiled Betty and if it had, had any change also been wrought in her? She was to find out in a very few minutes.

One Camp Fire law, that there was no escaping, was that the girls were not to spend but fifteen minutes in bathing. Really it hardly seemed like half that time before the four girls were once again on land getting into their bathing gowns which had been left hanging on a willow tree nearby. They were to dress later on in their tent, so they were hardly on shore more than a few moments, but even in that short space of time a noise a few yards away startled them. The four girls turned indignantly. In the entire week of their stay in camp they had not been disturbed by a single intruder. Sunrise Hill, with its tall pines - the emblem of the Camp Fire - its wooded lake for fishing, bathing and canoeing, and its utter seclusion, had seemed, after several weeks of careful search in the neighborhood about Woodford, the ideal place for the girls' summer camp. So far not even a friend, man or woman, had been allowed to visit them, because the camp was to be in running order before they received any outside criticism.

Now a young fellow of perhaps sixteen stood only a short distance off from the lake with an expression of superior amusement on his face. He was a country boy, for he wore no hat and his hair was burnt to a light straw color at the ends, his skin was almost bronze.

"Please go away," Polly demanded haughtily. She had gathered her bathing gown about her as though it were a Roman matron's robe and was feeling that her presence must be impressive although her hair was extremely wet and drops of water were trickling down her face.

However, the intruder paid not the least attention to her request, except to laugh as though her indignation gave him special pleasure. He was carrying a large tin pail on one arm and a basket on the other and of course his behavior was hardly that of a gentleman.

Anger for the moment kept Polly speechless, but a chorus of protests arose from Betty, Mollie and Esther. "We are camping here and we would rather not have visitors, so would you mind going back the way you have come?" Betty requested in her most Princess-like fashion.

"Not until I have seen the sights," the newcomer answered. He did not really look impertinent, only mischievous, and his eyes were as blue as Polly's.

"You don't suppose that I have walked a mile before breakfast and carried these heavy things except to find out what on the face of the earth you crazy girls are doing here, trying to pretend you are scouts or Indian squaws. Of all the foolishness!"

Perhaps even this short acquaintance with Polly O'Neill has suggested that she had, what is for some reason or other called an Irish temper, though temper does not belong wholly to Irish people. Polly herself did not know when this temper would take possession of her nor where it would lead her. At present the young man continued to walk slowly on toward the white tents, whistling to show his complete indifference, while the four girls could see that their friends were now stirring about in camp evidently getting ready to start breakfast.

Without reflecting Polly stooped. There on the ground before her lay a sharp rock, ground and polished by the waters of the lake, and like a shot from a bow she flung this stone whistling through the air at the intruder.

Whether she thought her stone would strike the young man or what particular effect her childish bad manners would have if it should, Polly herself did not know. However, she was startled and flushed hotly when, with an exclamation of pain, the boy put down his pail, placing one hand quickly to his head.

The four girls had started for their camp, but now Mollie, first flashing a look of surprise and scorn at her usually beloved sister, ran on ahead of the others. "I am so sorry," she said in a gentle, reserved manner peculiar to her, "you were rude not to go away when we asked you, but it is far worse for one of us to have been so childish as to strike you. I am dreadfully ashamed."

The young man smiled, not very cheerfully it must be admitted, but at least not looking so angry as he had the right to. 'Did you throw the stone?" he inquired. "I never would have believed a girl could throw straight if I hadn't felt the blow, so perhaps you are learning one or two things by living like boys. Never mind, I can see you are not the guilty one."

"We are not trying to live in the least like boys, only like sensible girls," Mollie started in to reply quietly, but the last part of her sentence trailed off into a faint whisper, for the young man had just taken his hand down from his head and his fingers were covered with blood, a few drops were even trickling down the back of his neck inside his soft flannel shirt.

The other three girls had now come close enough to see the blood also, and except for Betty, Pony would everlastingly have disgraced herself. There are many persons in the world whom the sight of blood fills with a strange shrinking and terror that is almost like faintness, and Polly was one of them. Now she wanted to run away, she even turned to fly, when her friend caught hold of her. "Don't be utterly stupid, Polly, you have done a foolish trick and you've got to face the music, for if you don't, you know Mollie is apt to take the blame upon herself."

Polly's knees were shaking and her thin expressive face so pale that she looked quite unlike herself. However, she managed to save a part of her dignity by saying with an attempt at a smile, as she stopped alongside Mollie and the young fellow, "I am sorry, I cannot tell a lie, I did it with my little hatchet, so please feel all the anger against me. I do hope I haven't hurt you very much."

The young man now stared at Polly and then at Mollie and afterwards back again from one to the other. He started to whistle but stopped himself in time. "Gee, but you are alike - with a difference," he returned, neither accepting nor refusing to accept Polly's half-hearted apology.

Hardly knowing why, except that the back of his neck was apparently covered with perspiration when there was no heat to explain it, the boy again put up his hand to his head. This time it was impossible to ignore the amount of blood that covered his hand nor the horrified faces of his small audience.

"I expect I can't go up to your camp, after all, when I am in such a fix, so you've come kind of close to getting your own way. I guess you, usually do!" he said, frowning up at Polly. "I wonder if it is too much to ask you girls to carry these things up to your tents; the pail has your morning's milk and is pretty heavy; the basket is only filled with strawberries. My father is the farmer who owns the land about here and I thought it would be a lark to find out what you campers were trying to do. Didn't mean anything serious but I guess you'll have to come for your own supplies after this as there ain't no one but me to bring 'em." He spoke rather churlishly, but then he did have cause.

"Hadn't you better wash your cut at the lake or come on up to the tent and let us do something there for you," Betty proposed, not knowing exactly what they should do in the present situation and yet feeling that something ought to be done. "I am afraid walking home in the sun with your head in that condition may make you ill."

The young man shook his head and then winced. "It ain't anything," he replied, beginning to back away, but at the same moment Mollie O'Neill took firm hold on his sleeve. "Come down to the water," she demanded quietly, "you are cut pretty badly, but I think I can stop the bleeding. I suppose the other girls will laugh at me, but ever since I have been in camp I have been carrying some gauze bandage about in my pocket and finding out what to do in case of accidents. I won't hurt you."

The young fellow had intended utterly to decline Mollie's kindly offer, but now her suggestion of not hurting amused him, besides he was sensible enough to know she was right. It was embarrassing, however, to have three other girls looking on during the operation, so whatever anguish Mollie caused him he felt prepared to endure in silence.

In a very business-like fashion the young girl drew her roll of surgeon's lint from an inside pocket of her bathing gown and a small pair of scissors. Then she made her patient sit down on the ground by the water's edge while she carefully examined his cut.

"I ought to help, Mollie," her sister suggested faintly, but Mollie shook her head and the young man appeared grateful. "I don't mind blood and you do, Polly," she returned, "besides if anybody is to help I would rather have Esther. I am afraid, if you don't mind, I have got to cut your hair away, it is already so matted with blood."

To almost any suggestion the patient would have agreed, since he had but one desire now, and that to get away from the strange girls about whom he had been so curious an hour before.

Mollie cheerfully snipped away several locks of his hair covering a space about as large as a dollar. The cut

Margaret Vandercook

she discovered was deeper than she had expected and, as it was still bleeding profusely, she next called Esther for advice. Very carefully then the two girls washed out the cut with clean water and then Mollie, finding a flat stone, made a pad by wrapping it a number of times with gauze. This she placed over the wound, binding the young man's head, Esther assisting in making the bandage as tight as he could endure.

All this time Polly, with Betty's hand firmly clutching hers, had stood quietly looking on at the scene. She was feeling penitent and ashamed, and yet her Irish sense of humor made her a little bit amused as well. Mollie was so entirely unconscious, but she did seem to be intensely enjoying her first opportunity to prove herself a worthy Camp Fire Girl.

Perhaps the young man vaguely felt Polly's amusement, although he did not look at her and certainly did not give her the satisfaction of knowing whether or not she had been forgiven. But he managed to thank Mollie and Esther more politely for what they had done for him, than his boorish manners earlier in the morning suggested, and even insisted on going on up to the camp with them in order to carry the heavy pail.

Several others of the Camp Fire girls, were by this time engaged in getting break fast and although they could hardly help showing surprise at the unexpected appearance of a wounded hero no questions were then asked.

Miss McMurtry did not seem annoyed at seeing the young man, indeed it turned out that she and several of the girls had walked over to Mr. Webster's farm the day before to ask as a special favor that milk be sent their camp each day. If she felt any displeasure, Betty and Polly were sure it was directed toward them, for the first week of Camp Fire life had not been altogether smooth and there were still adjustments to be made between some of the girls and their guardian.

CHAPTER VIII

OTHER GIRLS

Besides the four girls who have just returned from the lake there were six others in the camp at Sunrise Hill, their guardian, Miss McMurtry and one small imp or angel, according to one's way of looking at things. For Margaret Everett had joined the summer campers and, in order to accomplish it, had brought her small brother, Horace Virgil Everett, along with her. You see, the girls felt they simply must have Meg, so after a great deal of discussion it was decided that Horace Virgil would be an excellent person to practice mother craft upon and would certainly bring into service whatever first aid information might be required.

Meg was so gay, so sweet tempered and so utterly inconsequential. If things were going well in camp, if the sun was shining and everybody was feeling amiable then she was entirely happy, but if things were going wrong, then it was that Meg counted, for she kept her temper through almost any kind of stress. She did not have so many moods as Polly, she was not so quiet and reserved as Mollie, nor did she expect the world to move according to her desires, as Betty Ashton did. Meg's faults were that she was not a good manager and did try to do too many things at once and so did none of them well, but she had not had an easy time since her mother died two years ago. Although her father and older brother adored her, they were selfish in unconscious masculine ways, President Everett in devoting too much time to his school and John to his studies and amusements. Unfortunately neither of them realized that Meg might now and then grow weary of having a small brother, capable of originating new kind of mischief at least once an hour, everlastingly tagging after her. But Meg's cares (if she ever called them by that name) had for the present been entirely lifted from her, for she had ten other people now to help, her take care of "Bumps," whom the girls had rechristened "Hai-yi" or "Little Brother," and if Meg had been asked to vote upon the happiest week of her life since her mother's death she would instantly have voted her first week in camp with her own club of Camp Fire Girls.

Then there was Sylvia Wharton! Did Sylvia really enjoy the change in her life from staying cooped up in a great house, looked after by servants and alone a great part of the time when her father was away? Her brother Frank, who was several years older, seldom paid the least attention to her. If the little girl did enjoy the woods and the companionship of the other girls and all the opportunities that the camp fire life offered her, so far she showed not the slightest sign. Her one pleasure must have been her chance to haunt Polly O'Neill, for although she did not seem particularly happy when she was with Polly, certainly she never left her side unless she were compelled to do her share of the camp work and only then when Polly insisted upon it. Already Miss McMurtry felt that Sylvia might become difficult, but then the child had had no training, and besides Miss McMurtry shared the belief of almost all other persons that Sylvia was simply stupid. Curiously enough Eleanor Meade now appeared to have been invited into the first Woodford Camp Fire circle under a false impression. You see, the girls at the high school where Eleanor was also a student considered her a genius, and it is agreeable for a community to have one genius in its midst. Eleanor did have talent for drawing, and besides she had a number of characteristics which many persons associate with genius. She was entirely careless of her other responsibilities, and, if she happened to wish to paint, considered it entirely unreasonable that anything or anybody should interfere with her desire. She was often in the habit of forgetting engagements and at times there was a faraway expression in her eyes, which may have come from having neglected to wear her glasses, but which her friends believed due to the thrall of some wonderful creative idea which might be presented to the world some day in the form of a great picture. And Eleanor, being but human and seventeen, had done her best to foster this belief. She would not dress in modern fashions like the other girls; her parents had little money, but Eleanor's mother was a clever needlewoman and her eldest daughter always appeared in gowns made after exactly the same pattern and of some soft clinging material, whether cashmere or cheesecloth, they were always short waisted with a folded girdle and deep hem and cut low in the neck. Then Eleanor's hair, which was heavy and straight and a kind of ashen brown, was always worn parted in the middle and fixed in a great loose knot at the back of her neck. Eleanor was not pretty like Betty and Meg and Mollie and, at times, Polly O'Neill, but she would have scorned to have been thought pretty - interesting was the adjective she preferred.

However, since Eleanor's appearance in camp for

almost a week she had forgotten to be a genius. For one thing the girls were all wearing the regulation Camp Fire uniform, a loose blouse and dark blue serge skirt, and so she could not dress the part. Then, although the Camp Fire official log book had been given her to illustrate she had not even started to paint the totem of the Sunrise Camp on its brown leather cover, although Sunrise Hill stood, always before her in its changing beauty. The girls had taken its name for their camp with the thought that the hill might symbolize their own efforts to look upward always to the highest and most beautiful things.

But Eleanor should hardly be blamed for not having done much painting so far, there, had been such a lot of other work to do, in helping to put things in order in camp, and besides she had developed the most surprising talent for making an Irish stew, that was the envy and delight of all the other girls. Eleanor said it was because she had a soul above science and used her imagination in her stew, but whatever the reason, since the first day when the cooking of dinner fell to her, this stew had been one of the greatest successes in camp and Eleanor received her first honor bead for her genius in cooking instead of in art.

Besides these seven girls already described, there was an eighth girl in the Sunrise camp, the stranger whom Betty had brought home with her on the day their club had first been discussed - the girl whose face was so familiar to Mrs. Ashton but whose name was unknown. There had been a question as to whether or not this particular girl could come to summer camp, not because the other girls were unwilling to have her, but be se she worked in a milliner's shop in Woodford and had to go back and forth to be at work every day.

Quite by accident on the eventful afternoon Betty had stooped by this shop in her journey to Meg's to ask about her new spring hat, and being so full of her plan had poured it into Edith Norton's ear, while the little milliner was trying on her hat. Naturally Edith thought it a wonderful plan, so Betty, with one of her sudden impulses, immediately insisted that the young milliner come home with her to become a member of their new Camp Fire club. This seemed at the time a perfectly impossible dream to Edith, who was a poor girl with her own living to make, but then she did not understand Betty's ability to make things happen. Every obstacle had been smoothed away, Edith was now riding Betty's bicycle back and forth from camp to town every day and, already the headaches, which had first wakened Betty's sympathy, because of the pallor of her face and the dark circles under her eyes, had begun to grow better from the daily fresh air and exercise. Of the Camp Fire Girls Edith was the oldest; she was about eighteen and had blonde hair and delicate features, with brown eyes. She might have been pretty, but that she needed to grow stronger in body and character, and already the girls and their guardian had discovered that Edith was too fond of tea and coffee and sweets and modern novels for her own health or happiness. The trouble was that her home was too filled with small brothers and sisters and a father and mother too poor to make them comfortable, so that the eldest daughter had been forced to find her own pleasures.

The last two members of the Sunrise Hill camp were unknown to the other girls until a few days before. They were two sisters, daughters of a favorite doctor, cousin of Miss McMurtry's, who had been pupils in a fashionable boarding school in Philadelphia. They were not alike, either in appearance or character, for the older one of them thought too much about clothes and wealth and position, and so immediately fell to admiring and imitating Betty, while the other was an impossible tomboy, more like a feminine Puck, the very incarnation of mischief, whose one idea of happiness seemed to lie in playing pranks.

Juliet Field, the older girl, had light brown hair and eyes, was rather pretty and had a plump girlish figure, round fat cheeks with a good deal of color and a piquant, turned-up nose, while Beatrice, whom everybody called "Bee," wore her curly dark hair cut short, had a melancholy brown face entirely unlike her character and was as slender and small and quick in her movements as a tiny wren.

The two sisters and Sylvia Wharton slept in the tent with Miss McMurtry, while the third tent sheltered Eleanor, Edith, Meg and, of course, "little brother".

When Miss McMurtry had wakened to discover that four of the Camp Fire girls had gone in swimming without the others, she had not been pleased, more because she felt that Betty and Polly were too much inclined to be leaders among the girls and to disregard her advice. They had not yet openly disobeyed her, so of course she had been unable to say anything to them, but now she made up her mind to hang in each tent the rules for each day's camp routine so that there could be no more uncertainty. Miss McMurtry had merely been waiting to decide what rules were wisest before making her schedule.

As soon as their first masculine visitor departed Eleanor, Meg and Juliet announced breakfast. At a comfortable distance from the kitchen fire a large white cloth had been spread on the grass and in the center stood the great basket of fresh strawberries just brought over by the young man to whom Polly had given such an uncomfortable reception. A big coffee pot and two jugs of milk stood at opposite ends of the cloth besides toast and a dozen boiled eggs in a chafing dish, while from the nearby fire came the most delicious food odor in the world: bacon fried before open coals Nevertheless the girls did not sit down to breakfast at once although they were dreadfully hungry. Already they had established certain Camp Fire customs, and one was their morning habit of reciting some verse of thanksgiving in unison before beginning the real living of their day. The hymn, which first introduced Betty to Esther was always sung at the close of each day, but this morning verse had always to be original and one girl at a time was allowed to make the selection. To-day it had fallen to Polly's lot and she had taught it to the other girls over their camp fire the night before.

So now the ten girls with their guardian in the center stood in a semicircle facing Sunrise Hill. The sun had fully risen and the earth, as the Indians used to say, had "become white." Led by Polly they slowly recited this ancient chant:

"Shine on our gardens and fields, Shine on our working and weaving; Shine on the whole race of man, Believing and unbelieving; Shine on us now through the night, Shine on us now in Thy might, The flame of our holy love And the song of our worship receiving."

And when they had finished, Polly O'Neill, with a note of reverence in her voice that gave it an unconscious dramatic quality she would have vainly tried to have at any other time, added: "We Camp Fire girls worship not the fire but Him of whom in ages past it was the chosen symbol because it was the purest of all created things."

And then without further ceremony there was a sudden rush for breakfast.

CHAPTER IX

THE GUARDIAN

Miss Martha McMurtry was an odd guardian for a Camp Fire club which owed its existence to Betty Ashton's enthusiasm, for two more different persons cannot well be imagined. Of course the girls in the club were of many kinds and characters and it would have been almost impossible for any guardian to have been congenial with all of them, but it was unfortunate that the head of the Sunrise Camp and the two girls who were its leading spirits had at the beginning of the summer so little in common. For there was no question but that Betty and Polly were leaders, one week in camp had been more than sufficient to prove this.

Betty's influence was of course easy to understand, for she was uncommonly pretty and wealthy, and though spoiled and wayward, given to sudden generous impulses and affections which made her friends willing to overlook her faults. With Polly, O'Neill the case was different, she had no money and was not particularly good looking, it was simply that the intensity of her emotions would always, whether as a woman or child, make her a force for good or evil. When Polly was happy persons about her found it almost impossible not to share in her mood, she had such a delicious sense of humor and was so full of clever jokes and delicate, unconscious flatterings. Then when an ugly mood descended upon her, and, as Polly in Irish fashion used to say, "a witch rode on her shoulders," it was almost equally impossible to ignore her foolishly tragic points of view. There is an old name for Ireland, Innis Fodhla, which means the Island of Destiny, and though Polly had been born in a little New England village, nevertheless, in her blood there was a strain of those inheritances which have made the Irish nation so unlike all others.

While Betty and Polly were friends there was apt to be peace among all the girls in camp, but if they should disagree? Ah well, they had never really had any serious differences of opinion in their lives which Mollie, after the passing of a day or two, had not been able to smooth over. And they both had every intention of making themselves as agreeable as possible to their guardian.

Of course from the beginning of things it had been perfectly apparent that Betty would never voluntarily have chosen Miss McMurtry for their camp guardian, but finding that her science teacher was the only woman in Woodford who knew about the Camp Fire movement and was able to spend the summer with them, she had accepted the situation with as good a grace as possible.

Miss Martha McMurtry was not an attractive woman when she first came into the Sunrise Camp. Names have an odd fashion of describing the persons who own them and Miss McMurtry's exactly described her. Have you not a mental picture of a tall, learned young woman, with straight black hair, which she wore pulled back very tight, forming an unattractive knot at the back of her head? Of course she also wore glasses, having spent all her life inside of books until her pupils were convinced that she knew everything in the world. She did know a great deal and because of her knowledge was a splendid Camp Fire guardian, but there were a few things about human nature which her girls were to teach her in exchange for her science. Her information covered a number of fields, for while she taught botany and chemistry at the Girls' High School, she had also taken a two years' course in domestic science before beginning her teaching. Miss McMurtry was only twenty-six, had no family and lived all alone in a small house in Woodford. However, she appeared much older, and one of the questions her pupils were never able to answer was whether she had ever had a man call on her in her life. About her early history there was very little known, as she did not care to talk about herself and no one asked about her past.

About five o'clock on the next afternoon Miss McMurtry and Esther Clark were seated not far from a small fire which they had lately built near their pine grove. The day was not cold, but New Hampshire is seldom very warm in June and, besides, no one in camp ever tried to resist the opportunity for having a fire when most of their pleasure in being in camp centered around it.

Back and forth from the pine grove to his friends Hai-ya, Little Brother, traveled. He was cheerfully engaged in bringing pine cones to Miss McMurtry, and piling them into a small mound, later to be thrown on the fire. On the ground between the woman and girl were some odd pieces of khaki galatea, bits of leather fringe, shells and beads, and Esther was busily sewing. Miss McMurtry was writing: several times she had torn up what she had written, throwing the waste paper into the fire, but finally she handed a sheet to Esther in a hesitating way.

"See what you think of this, Esther?" she asked. "You see the Camp Guardians are advised to follow certain rules and regulations in camp life and I have been trying to decide what would best suit us. Please tell me what you think?"

Esther looked the paper over thoughtfully, and then began reading it aloud.

6:30 A.M. Arise, wash, either bathing in lake or tent, then air bedding thoroughly. Hoist American flag, salute it. Three girls prepare breakfast.

7:30 A.M. Recite in unison morning verse, eat breakfast, make up own bed and clean tent, also do whatever share of work is apportioned for the day.

10 to 12 A.M. Devote to practice in one of the seven Camp Fire crafts for obtaining honors.

12 to 1 P.M. Three girls prepare dinner.

1 to 2 P.M. Dinner served.

2 to 3 P.M. Rest.

3 to 5:30 P.M. Recreation.

5:30 to 6:30 P.M. Three girls prepare tea.

6:30 to 7 P.M. Tea served.

7:00 to 8:30 P.M. Camp Fire, stories, songs, confidences, etc.

8:30 P.M. Milk and crackers, bed.

9 P.M. Lights out.

Ester read the schedule over the second time and then nodded her head approvingly. "It's splendid and I am sure the girls will think it can't be improved upon," she answered, adding the latter part of her speech as she handed the paper back, for Miss McMurtry was looking troubled and Ester half guessed the cause.

Miss McMurtry said nothing, however, only picking up a piece of Ester's sewing.

"What is this you're making, Ester?" she inquired. "I thought you had made your ceremonial Camp Fire dress some time ago!"

Ester did not reply at once as she bent more closely over her work, but on being asked the question the second time returned with an attempt at speaking carelessly: ' Oh, it's Betty's costume, I hope you won't mind, but she says really she never has had time to do any sewing since our club was formed. So, as we are to have our June Council Fire to-night, I promised to finished it for her. You see this is our most important meeting because that afternoon in town we did not have an opportunity to arrange appropriate ceremonies."

Miss McMurtry nodded, "Yes, but I thought it was part of our plan to have each girl make her own dress. Even Sylvia Wharton has done her best to help."

Miss McMurtry picked up a portion of the neglected dress, however, and began to assist Esther. "I wonder if it is a good thing for you and Betty to be together," she remarked thoughtfully. "Of course I know Mrs. Aston's intentions were for the best in taking you to live with them at this late date and they will probably be very kind to you, but really there isn't any reason, Esther, why you should take all the cares away from Betty. She seems to be one of the persons in the world for whom nothing is ever made difficult, while you - " Breaking off abruptly she turned to see if her small charge was still busy and then shaded her eyes from the sun.

Esther laughed happily. Not so shy and awkward here in the woods with the other girls, she had lately thought little of her own lack of advantages. "You needn't worry about me," she now replied, stopping her work for a moment to look off across the fields for the return of the other Camp Fire Girls. "Already I perfectly adore Betty. Of course she does not care a great deal for me, for there is nothing in me to attract her, but all my life I have wanted some one to love, and sort of take care of and do things for. Of course Betty has so many people she does not need me much now, but some day. Oh well, as she herself says, one never can tell just how things may turn out in this world."

"Wohelo, Wohelo, Wohelo!" A far cry from several voices sounded across the fields and a few moments later Betty Ashton, Meg, Eleanor and Juliet Field came into view. Betty was wearing her every day Camp Fire costume with the official hat of blue cloth embroidered with a silver gray "W" on a dark red background and over her shoulder was strapped a smart knapsack. She seemed to dance away from the other girls, although she was not dancing but running. Yet such was her grace and slenderness that somehow she appeared:

Like to a lady turning in the dance, Foot before foot from earth so slightly moved, That scarce perceptible her advance.

Arriving first she threw herself down on the ground near Esther, tossing off her hat and resting her head on the other girl's lap.

"I am nearly dead!" she exclaimed rather irritably. "Two miles walk into town and two miles back is a good deal when one has been doing a thousand things beforehand. Besides, I didn't find a letter from mother or father, and Mollie and Polly have seven from Mrs. O'Neill, one for each day of her trip from New York to Queenstown. Of course it does take longer for a ship to land in Naples, so I am silly to be disappointed, yet I am just the same! Besides, Polly was dreadfully obstinate and would insist on coming back to camp by another route, said it was shorter and much more adventurous than the open road. So we parted, and Mollie and Sylvia and Bee axe returning with her. She may be having more adventures than we did, but the way is not shorter, for we appear to have arrived first."

Opening her knapsack Betty then handed two letters to Miss McMurtry and gave a little rolled package to Esther. "Here is something for you from Dick; he doesn't seem to have written me either."

Esther unwrapped her parcel. "It is just a piece of music your brother told me about, an Indian love song. He thought perhaps I could learn it and we could sing it together in camp. He is very kind."

Betty shrugged her shoulders. "Oh yes, Dick is kind to nearly everybody, except to me sometimes when he thinks I need discipline. But he and mother both think you have a remarkable voice, Esther, and that it will be a pity if you don't have it cultivated some day."

Esther laughed, touching Betty's auburn hair affectionately. It was loosened from her walk and curling round her face. "That is my soul's desire, Betty," she whispered, surprised at her sudden burst of confidence. But Betty's manner with her was unexpectedly more intimate than it had been since their first meeting. She could hardly have known that it was owing to the fact that she had just quarreled with her adored Polly. Of course Betty did not intend to be deceitful, she was simply in the habit of seeking consolation from some source, whenever things went wrong with her.

Now she put her hand the second time into her knapsack and, drawing forth a square white box, she proceeded to open it in a slightly shamefaced fashion and then handed it to Miss McMurtry. "I am a dreadful backslider from Camp Fire rules, but I just had to have some candy this afternoon. Do eat some with me, so I won't be the only sinner in camp," she begged.

Miss McMurtry shook her head. "Don't tempt Esther or any of the other girls, Betty," she replied in a tone that Betty was familiar with at school. "One of the health craft rules you girls have promised to observe is to give up candy between meals for three months. Of course if you wish to break your word you may, but I had rather you would not try to influence any one else."

Betty banged the lid back on her box.

"Oh," she replied unsteadily. "I am sorry you feel about me in that way. I didn't mean to be a mischief maker, but you need not worry about Esther, for she is not the kind that falls from grace."

She sat a few moments longer leaning her chin on her hand and looking toward the grove of pine trees where the shadows were now growing longer and darker as the afternoon lengthened. Sorry to have fallen from grace herself, Betty at this moment would have perished rather than confess it.

The other three girls had gone straight on up to the tents, Meg taking "Little Brother" with her. But now Eleanor appeared at the opening before their kitchen tent and began vigorously ringing a large dinner bell.

"Betty Ashton," she called, "it is half-past five o'clock and time to begin dinner. You know it is your turn to help with Juliet and me. Meg is putting the baby to bed."

Betty encircled her hand above her lips forming a small trumpet. "I am not going to help with dinner to-night, I am too dead tired," she halloed back. "I will help to-morrow instead."

"To-morrow?" Eleanor cried indignantly. "What has to-morrow, got to do with it? You are no more tired than the rest of us and besides it is your turn to-night and we have promised not to try to get out of things unless we are ill." Eleanor said nothing more, but even at a distance of a good many yards it was plain that she had flounced back inside the tent. When she came out again with some pots and pans her air was one of conscious and offended virtue.

A moment later Betty sighed. "I wonder if you would mind taking my place this afternoon, Esther?" she inquired. "I am very tired and you haven't been doing anything. Would you mind, Miss Martha?"

Betty made her request very prettily and really without the least idea that it could be refused, for she was not in the habit of being made to do what she did not wish. With her own family to have said she was tired would have been regarded as a sufficient excuse for any change of plan.

Perhaps Miss McMurtry would have been wiser had she agreed to Betty's request, and had she been another girl she possibly might have been more lenient. Now she decided that Betty was simply trying to shirk her responsibilities and so slowly shook her head.

"Of course if you are not well, Betty, I will be glad to take your place myself," she answered, trying to speak kindly. "However, if I were you, I would hardly say that Esther has been doing nothing since she has been sewing all afternoon on the ceremonial dress you promised to make your self, so that you may wear it to our Council Fire to-night."

Betty got up quickly. "Please don't do any further work for me while we are in camp together, Esther," she demanded, "for it is evident that Miss McMurtry thinks I spend my time trying to impose upon you. As far as the dress is concerned, I shall not need it to-night, for I shall not come to the Council Fire. I will do my part in helping to get dinner, of course, but I prefer to rest afterwards."

Hardly, knowing what she was doing because of her anger, Betty yet managed to get up quietly from her place and start toward camp without glancing at either Esther or Miss McMurtry, although she heard Esther following close behind her. "Please don't disappoint us, dear," Esther pleaded. "I know Miss Martha will be willing to let me do your work to-night, if we ask her again, and it will quite ruin our Council Fire if you are not with us. What will Polly say when you and she have planned the whole ceremony? And I - I shall be so disappointed, for I am to be made a Fire-Maker to-night. Besides, you know we are to talk over the names we hope to be known by in our club."

But Betty only walked steadily on as though deaf to the other girl's entreaty. Near her own tent she turned at last and Esther could see that her eyes were full of tears. "You are mistaken, Esther, though I am sure you are very kind," she insisted with her offended Princess air, about which Polly used so often to tease her. "I am sure no one will miss me in the least and my absence will give you a chance to bestow on me the title you think really belongs to me, such as: 'Betty who won't bear her own burdens' or anything you prefer. Please leave me alone now."

So there was nothing more for Esther to do but to return to her work, knowing how little influence she had with Betty at any time.

CHAPTER X

PIPES OF PEACE

Half an hour later Polly discovered Esther seated alone by her slowly perishing fire taking the last stitches in Betty's rejected ceremonial dress. She had even embroidered on the left sleeve a small crown in gold colored silk, since Betty's old title "The Princess" would scarcely be changed whatever new names might be awarded to the other girls in their Camp Fire.

"Where's Betty?" Polly inquired carelessly. "I hope she wasn't cross; I suppose it was not kind of me to leave her and return another way, and she was right, it did make us late, but we had a delicious adventure!" Polly had dropped down on the ground and put her arms about her, knees, slowly rocking herself back and forth, her face shining with mischief and excitement, so that her color came and went quickly and tiny sparks appeared to dart forth from the blueness of her eyes and the blackness of her hair.

But as Esther neither answered nor asked any questions Polly stared at her in amazement. She had no particular emotion for Esther one way or the other, perhaps because she was not yet a rival in Betty's affections, but she had always tried to make herself agreeable to her and to have her feel like one of them;

moreover, she did not enjoy being disregarded.

Halfway up on her feet a glance at Esther's face made her drop back into her old position, except that she put one hand under the girl's chin, turning her face toward her.

"For goodness' sake, Esther, what is the matter?" she demanded. "I suppose it is Betty!"

And Esther nodded, feeling an absurd disposition to shed actual tears of disappointment. So much had been planned for to-night's Council Fire and this was the first disagreement in their camp. Should Betty fail to appear, the other girls, learning the cause, were sure to take sides and no one would be really happy.

Until Esther finished her story Polly listened without comment, although her face flushed and her lips were pressed close together.

"I do think Miss McMurtry was a little hard," she said finally. "It isn't fair to expect us to reform all at once and she might remember that Betty has never had the discipline of having to do things when she didn't wish to before. It is different when one has been poor, isn't it, Esther? Never mind, I will do my best. Betty hasn't any right to make everybody uncomfortable just because she is offended, particularly when she has had so much to do with our plans for to-night."

Polly disappeared, but when tea was served a short time later a signal to Esther reported that she had met with no success. Betty helped with the evening work, saying nothing but looking pale and tired, so that Miss McMurtry wondered if she had been too severe.

Perhaps Betty was used up by her walk! She would have liked to have talked to her but had no opportunity, for as soon as supper was over (and three other girls always did the clearing up) Betty immediately disappeared inside her tent, and when her three friends came in to dress for their meeting they found her in bed covered up with her blue blankets and not in the mood for conversation.

Vainly Mollie and Esther attempted persuasion, reproaches, they received always the same answer - fatigue and not ill temper kept Betty from their entertainment. She was sorry of course but they would probably have a better time without her.

Curious, but in the half hour required by the three girls for their dressing, Polly, in spite of her promise, added not a single word of regret or entreaty in spite of Esther's pleading looks and Mollie's outspoken demands that her sister exert her influence. Appearing utterly absorbed in her own costume and in admiring Esther's and Mollie's, Polly only shook her head.

The June afternoon was a long one, so there still remained sufficient daylight for the girls to see to dress in their tent. Over the crest of Sunrise Hill a pale crescent moon with a single star glowing beneath it had now arisen and the moonlight later on promised to be radiant.

There were bursts of laughter, cries of admiration floating from one open tent to the other, for this was the first time the girls had seen one another dressed in their new costumes.

Polly plaited her long black hair in two braids, twining

Margaret Vandercook

it in and out with narrow strips of bright orange ribbon, and then around her head she bound a broader band of ribbon the, same color with a single black feather just above her forehead on the left side. With her dark hair and high cheek bones, which to-night were crimson with excitement, she made an unusually picturesque Indian girl. Mollie's hair was softer in texture and less heavy, so that she wore it hanging loose over her shoulders.

At first, however, Esther's appearance was not much of a success. Although, apparently lost in languor and uninterested in anything, from her couch Betty observed her, wondering what could be done. For Esther to look so awkward and plain to-night, when as the first of their Camp Fire girls to be raised to the rank of Fire Maker she would be the center of all eyes, did seem hardly fair.

Trying to make the best of herself and without the gift most girls have in this direction, Esther had also arranged her hair in two braids, but while her hair was thick it was too short to be effective in this style, and parted in the middle accentuated the plainness of her long face with its irregular features, light blue eyes and large mouth; moreover, the bright yellow of her khaki costume with its red fringes, gay shell and beads made her complexion appear in contrast paler than ever. In despair she was twisting a band of bright red cotton decorated in brass spangles about her forehead, when a cry from Polly, who happened at this moment to catch sight of her, made her drop her head-dress.

"Stop, and don't you ever so long as you live, Esther Clark, dare to put a touch of red near your face," Polly demanded autocratically, rummaging at the same time in a small box on a table which she knew held a number of trinkets belonging to Betty. The next moment drawing forth a band of dull silver embroidery about an inch and a half wide, she crossed over to the older girl.

"Please let me fix you a little differently," she urged coaxingly, beginning at once to unwind Esther's hair and combing it out over her shoulders; then loosening it in front she put the silver band like a crown about it. Esther's hair wag red, of this there could be no denial, but now unbound it showed bright strands of gold and darker shades of red that could never have been discovered when tightly fastened to her head. Perhaps it was partly due to Polly's little act of friendliness making the other girl happier, but certainly there was a marked change for the better in Esther's appearance, so much so that Betty decided she looked almost pretty when a few moments afterwards her three friends bidding farewell to her went out leaving her alone in her tent, where the darkness was now closing in. In parting, Mollie and Esther had added a final plea to Betty to join them, but still Polly had spoken no word.

Lying alone on her couch Betty wondered why? Of course Polly was always being swept off her feet by new people and new interests and so after ten days in camp would not be so fond of her, but it was odd that she cared nothing for her presence at their Council Fire to-night, since they had planned the whole ceremony together and were to play leading parts.

Partly to close out the moonlight, which was now shining faintly inside her tent, and partly to shut her ears to the voices and laughter of her friends, Betty turned over on her balsam pillow with her face to the tent side, and there covering up her head lay perfectly still, so still that she would not even put her handkerchief to her eyes, although for some reason or other they were uncomfortably moist.

Fifteen minutes passed and there was no noise of a returning footfall, but presently there was a faint, sweet odor in the lodge and Betty heard a low call such as a boy would make on a wild reed whistle.

She did not stir, so the sound was repeated more shrilly, and by and by a pair of hands forcibly pulled the blankets down from her face.

There stood Polly in her Indian costume with her intense love for the dramatic shining in her eager face and holding above Betty's head two perforated sticks, one painted blue to represent the sky, the other green to represent the earth, and both of them decorated in tiny feathers of birds and a pair of wing-like pendants.

"Betty," Polly asked quietly, "do you remember the names of these two Indian treasures and how hard we have worked to make them as like the originals as we could?"

"Of course, they are the calumets you are to use in the Council Fire ceremony to-night. They are pretty!" Betty conceded.

But Polly had dropped down by the side of her bed. "They have another name, Betty, which isn't calumets and you know it, and we were to use them at our Council Fire to-night. They are called 'pipes of peace' and I can't very well lead the party that is to bring them to camp and also the children who are to receive them."

A silence in the tent then followed, lasting several moments.

"Aren't you a little ashamed, Princess, thinking of the character of our ceremony this evening, not to be willing to be present? It is to be war and not peace then, isn't it?"

Betty laughed. "I only said I was tired," she argued faintly. "I am sure no one has the least reason for thinking I am angry if I happen to prefer to rest."

Then Polly began to feel that her case was won. Very quietly she slipped over to a wooden dress-good's box covered with bright cretonne and, opening it, drew forth the ceremonial dress so recently finished by Esther, then she lighted two candles on either side the table underneath their small mirror. Betty's head-dress was there, a band of her favorite blue velvet ribbon with three white feathers crossed in front. Catching it up Polly waved it temptingly.

"Come on, Betty, and let me help you dress, everybody is waiting for us and there never was such a night!" But seeing that her friend still hesitated, added in a tone which was a question, not a reproach: "Don't you think, dear, that so long as you really originated our Camp Fire club and asked Miss McMurtry to be our guardian, it is rather a pity for you to make the first break? Isn't one of the Camp Fire ideas to learn to put the happiness of a good many people before our own personal desires?"

In a half minute Betty was out of bed with her Camp

Fire dress nearly on. "If you are going to turn preacher and reform at this time of life, Polly O'Neill, then goodness knows what is to become of me! Once you were my partner in crime, but now - well, it is hard to think of you even yet as 'Saint Polly'!"

"And will be to the end, me darling," Polly agreed, dropping into her Irish brogue from sheer pleasure that her purpose was accomplished.

Five minutes later the two friends were hurrying forth toward a circular piece of ground some yards from their tent, which to-night the girls wished known as their "earth lodge." There the other Camp Fire members had already assembled with a great pile of wood in their midst waiting to be kindled.

CHAPTER XI

UNDER THE ROSE MOON

In June the moon of the Camp Fire girls is known as the Rose Moon. But there were no roses blooming near their camping grounds at Sunrise Hill to-night and only the odor of the pines made the night air fragrant.

Betty went straight up to Miss McMurtry, however, and in her hand carried a small cluster of pink roses.

"I brought you these from our garden at home this afternoon; the house is closed, but our old gardener is miserable because no one is about to enjoy his flowers. Please wear them."

Then before the older woman could do more than murmur "Thank you," Betty had slipped away and taken her place in the circle of girls between Meg and Esther, not without noticing, however, that their guardian looked unusually well in a dress of plain white serge with her dark hair bound about her head like a coronet. Also she saw that Miss McMurtry's face had brightened, as she placed the flowers in her belt and felt that peace was restored between them even before the beginning of their ceremony of peace.

The little company had evidently been waiting for the

Margaret Vandercook

appearance of Betty and Polly, for now Miss McMurtry stepped into the center of their group and there was instant silence. She looked slowly about at the ten faces gazing upon her with rapt attention and then sang in a low tone, and yet one that could be distinctly heard, this ancient Indian chant.

"To-day our Father (Sun) shone into our lodge, his power is very strong, To-night our mother (Moon) shines into our lodge, her power is very strong, I pray the Morning Star (their Son) that when he rises at daybreak, he too will shine in to bless us and give us long life."

This chant signified the opening of the Council Fire. For the next moment Miss McMurtry turned toward the heap of wood carefully placed in the center of the circle, by the wood-gatherers. A little pile of paper with some small chips and dried twigs on top of it lay on the ground, above which leaned a pyramid of larger logs, waiting to be lighted.

Kneeling close by this pile the guardian of the Sunrise Camp Fire took from her pocket a bit of flint and a piece of steel, striking them sharply together. Tiny sparks flew forth but no answering crackle resounded from the wood and paper, although the sparks darted in and out among them like miniature fireflies. Once more Miss McMurtry tried her flint and steel according to the prescribed rules, but again the result was failure.

Of course matches were not a luxury at Sunrise Camp and in the making of their daily fires the campers were not superior to the using of them, but this lighting of their first real Council Fire was to be a truly important ceremony and greatly the members desired to return to the primitive method of fire-making.

There must be something more than superstition in the old axiom that the third time is charm, perhaps three efforts are required for the training of the human will; but however that may be, at the third striking together of the metal and the flint the Sunrise Council fire sprang into life, stick by stick it blazed forth, until at last a tongue of flame leaping up in the air encircled the whole pyramid, setting the pine logs into a splendid flare.

On ten different faces it shone, revealing as many characters when, seated in Indian fashion on straw mats upon the ground, the Camp Fire girls now repeated in unison their "Ode to Fire."

"Oh, Fire! Long years ago when our fathers fought with great animals you were their protection. From the cruel cold of winter, you saved them. When they needed food you changed the flesh of beasts into savory meat for them. During all the ages your mysterious flame has been a symbol to them for Spirit. So (to-night) we light our fire in remembrance of the Great Spirit who gave you to us."

Then Polly slowly arose from her place, approached the flames and cast upon them a great bunch of sweet dried grass; a moment later the rising smoke filled the air with an odor like incense.

But the chief feature of to-night's ceremony was to be the elevation of Esther Clark to the rank of Fire-Maker. For three months had she been working to gain the fourteen necessary requirements and the twenty elective honors, yet now as the moment for receiving her reward drew near she felt a strong disposition to run away. Betty must have guessed her feeling, for at the critical moment she slipped her arm through the older girl's, smiling at her and pressing her hand encouragingly.

"Don't be foolish and don't be frightened, Esther," she whispered encouragingly, "for you are only to receive the honor that is your just due!"

Curious how often in the years that would follow, these same simple words of Betty's were to be repeated in almost the same form to the girl now seated at her side!

Seeing that Esther was too timid to approach the center of the circle alone, Betty accompanied her, standing a little to one side, while Esther, in order to show her complete understanding of the whole Camp Fire idea, repeated once again in her low beautiful voice (almost her only attraction at this time of her life) "The Firemaker's Desire," the same verse she had recited to Betty Ashton over her own fire on the day of their first meeting in the Ashton home. Then Miss McMurtry slipped over Esther's head a string of twenty shining beads representing her new honors, and amid much clapping of hands from their small audience the two girls returned to their places, Esther wondering if she were not almost as happy in Betty's companionship as in her new title. For remember, she had never had any intimate tie in her life, no father or mother, no sisters or brothers, and only the care and kindness of strangers until Miss McMurtry had made of her a friend.

All this time Polly O'Neill has been vainly trying to pretend that she is devoutly interested in what is taking place, although any one knowing her would have understood that Polly's real attention was absorbed in the feature of their Council Fire ceremony in which she was to play the leading role. Now without further delay, and followed by Meg, Eleanor, Beatrice and the faithful Sylvia, she disappeared into the Pine grove not far from the gathering of the Council, while the remaining girls and their guardian drew nearer to their own fire, heaping it with fresh pine branches.

And by and by, from the edge of the trees, the same notes from the reed-like whistle that had called Betty to her place in the ceremony of peace, now about to take place, were repeated. Then along a white path of moonlight, in their Indian costumes, the five girls led by Polly, swaying her pipes of peace slowly above her head, came dancing with a queer, rhythmical movement of their bodies, arms and feet.

A strange spectacle for these modern days, and yet many such an Indian dance had taken place in these same New England hills hundreds of years before!

As they drew near enough to be plainly seen by the little party waiting in their "earth lodge," Betty got up from her place, lifting on high a fluttering white handkerchief tied to a birch pole.

In the old days there were always two parties to this ancient Indian ceremony of peace: those bringing the calumets were called "the fathers" and those receiving them "the children". So it was necessary that Betty should now indicate that "the children" were willing to receive the blessing the other party desired to bring.

The five visiting girls stood facing those seated on the

ground; Polly standing before their guardian and still waving her blue and green perforated sticks made her carefully memorized speech with the dramatic intensity dear to her theatrical soul.

"These pipes of peace once symbolized heaven and earth to the Indians and the mysterious power that permeates all nature. In their presence the Indians were taught to care for their children, to think of the future welfare of their people and to live at peace with one another. The Indians were supposed to be a savage race and yet their prayer seems to come very near to the ideals of the Camp Fire girls. May we also live in peace with one another, learning from the women of the past all that was best in their lives and refitting it to the needs of the now women of to-day and to-morrow."

Then at the end of her invocation she moved quietly from one Camp Fire girl to the other, waving her blessing of peace over each bowed head. And as she moved she sang the Indian song of peace, the other girls straightway joining in, but it was not Polly's voice but Esther's that carried the music of the refrain far out over the fields, carried it at last to the ears of some one who had been seeking the home of the Sunrise Camp for the past two hours.

"Down through the ages vast On wings strong and true, From great Wa-kon-da comes Good will to you - Peace that shall here remain."

CHAPTER XII

NAN

At the close of the calumet ceremony the girls immediately drew closer together about the fire, making ready for an informal discussion. Of course they had been uncommonly serious for the past hour, but the night was so mystically beautiful with the new moon casting a silver radiance over the hills and fields, that there in the yellow glow of the Council Fire the girls had felt the inspiration of its beauty and their own seclusion.

Since darkness had fallen there had been no noise save the murmur of their own voices and the cry of "Hinakaga", the owl, like a sentry at his post making his report from the grove of pines.

Once or twice as the time slipped away Miss McMurtry had faintly suggested that the hour had come for retiring, but always the girls, led by Polly O'Neill, had pleaded that to-night was not like other nights, and they must be allowed a slightly longer respite. During the earlier part of the evening, when she had believed no one observing her, Polly had evidently been on the lookout for something or some one, for she had kept glancing slyly out across the country toward the path leading to their camp; now, however, this idea must have passed from her mind, for she was as completely absorbed as her companions in the selection of the new names, which the girls might hope to bear in their Camp Fire club.

Miss McMurtry talked very little - persons who are deep students rarely do; far more apt are those of us who play upon the surface of life to like to do our thinking aloud. So now, the Council was surprised to hear her speak in so earnest a tone that every one else was silenced:

"Girls, I want you to do me a favor to-night. I don't know whether it is usual for the guardian of a Camp Fire club to have a new title awarded her, but nevertheless I want you to give me one. You see I am Miss Martha or Miss McMurtry to most of you at school and really I wish to forget that I am a schoolmarm this summer and to have you forget it. I have been finding out a good many things since I came into camp, though it hasn't been very long, and one of them is that a guardian does not need so much to be a teacher as a friend to her girls. You see no guardian can know everything that you girls are studying to gain your elective honors, but, if we are friends we can work them out together."

Deeply grateful was Betty Ashton for the night and the shadows of the firelight that were playing on her face while Miss McMurtry was making this little speech, which she could hardly help knowing was directed in a large measure to her. However, she could not refrain from giving Esther's arm a knowing pinch and then raising her eyes to intercept a returning glance from Polly.

Possibly Miss McMurtry expected Betty's point of view, even if she did not see her express her surprise, for although some distance away from her place in the circle her next remark was addressed to Betty.

"Betty, can't you think of a name for me?" she asked deliberately, wondering what answer under the circumstances she would be apt to receive. "I know you and Polly have been reading a good deal in order to find new names to suggest to the girls, so haven't you come across a name that might be suitable for me? There are astrologers and fortune tellers who believe that one's good or evil fate depends on bearing an appropriate name and I have always hated mine."

"But it exactly suits you and doesn't make you ridiculous like my name does me!" Sylvia Wharton announced unexpectedly, breaking into the conversation for the first time during the evening in her dull, even tones. "What is really horrid is to have a name that suggests some one very beautiful and graceful - a name that sounds like water running over pebbles in a brook and then to look like I do. I wish everybody would call me Mary Jane! I would like to have a plain, homely name."

Such was the astonishment following Sylvia's protest that no one spoke for at least half a minute. Who could have supposed her capable of developing so much of an idea? For once in their acquaintance Polly (for of course Sylvia managed to be next her) laughed with the little girl instead of at her, at the same time taking the trouble to give one of her stiff flaxen braids an amused tug, while Miss McMurtry, in order to break the silence, went on talking about herself.

"Of course my name suits me, Sylvia, that is the worst of it," she laughed. "How can any one named Martha escape being a Martha? Oh, I presume the name taken by itself is a good old-fashioned one, but in combination with McMurtry it has such an old-maidy, school-teachery sound that I have been compelled to live up to it. Now, Betty, please make a suggestion."

Betty flushed and at the same time smiled to herself. The Indian name "Pokamp" or catbird had come to her mind shortly after her quarrel with Miss McMurtry during the afternoon. "Minerva," she now proposed faintly, "she was the Goddess of Wisdom."

"Gracious no, that is worse than Martha to live up to!" Miss McMurtry objected and also declined just as decisively the dignity of "Hypatia" and "Aspasia', when those learned ladies of ancient times were offered for her consideration.

"We might call you 'Our Lady Protector'; it is just another expression for guardian," Mollie O'Neill proposed uncertainly, not because she had any enthusiasm for her idea but because no one else had anything better to introduce, but before Miss McMurtry could answer, Polly's laugh had settled the proposition.

"Or we might call Miss Martha 'Chest Protector' or 'Bella Donna Plaster', which is a very soothing title, meaning 'Beautiful Lady Covering'," she teased. "Suppose, Miss Martha, that we just wait and perhaps follow the old Indian custom of choosing your name through a dream or the first object we see at an appointed time. But I must be allowed to bestow Mollie's new name upon her," she added, gazing sentimentally up into the sky and putting her arm apologetically about her sister, riot knowing how much she might have enjoyed being laughed at in public.

This time, however, it was Mollie who plainly scored, for she only laughed good humouredly saying: "Go ahead, Polly, you have arranged everything else for me in my life except my name and you only didn't do that at baptism because you were but a few weeks old!"

During the shouts of merriment, Polly, acknowledging her autocratic tendencies, could only hide her diminished head on her sister's shoulder; nevertheless, sitting up again a few moments later she pointed one hand in a dramatic fashion toward the heavens. "Only hear the name I have found for you and you will forgive me much, Mollie Mavourneen," she pleaded. "It is a part of our Camp Fire education to study the stars, isn't it? Well, see the Seven Brothers, the Great Bear family forming the Big Dipper in the northern sky. How many of us know that those stars were shot up there to escape the wrath of their terrible brother, Grizzly Bear, according to Indian astronomy. Now see that small star just at one side of the handle of the Dipper, known as 'Sinopa'. Don't you think we ought to call Mollie, 'Sinopa,' when it means 'Little Sister'?"

Overwhelmed by the general approval of Polly's suggestion, Mollie would never have had the courage to oppose it, but fortunately had no such desire and so as usual agreed to her sister's wishes.

"Marjoram" the girls next voted an appropriate new name for Margaret Everett if she needed one, because in the first place the word was like her own name and more important was its pretty German meaning, "happy-minded", one of those rare plants that has no single ugly quality.

Edith Norton agreed to be called "Apoi-a-kimi," because the Indian word meant "light hair" and she was particularly proud of her own fluffy blonde hair even though since becoming a Camp Fire girl she had felt compelled to hide away her puffs.

Very easily might the girls have continued this discussion of their titles until the sun rose beyond their Sunrise Hill, had not Miss McMurtry suddenly looked at her watch by bending close to the light of their fire. Then she rose so quickly and with such a sharp exclamation of surprise that several of the girls got up with her.

"Camp Fire maidens, what are we thinking of? It is after ten o'clock and we must say good-night and extinguish our fire. What a wonderful night it has been, so quiet, so serene that I think no one of us will soon forget it!" Very naturally she looked away from the group of girls close about her for a wider view of the landscape, hoping that this vision of its beauty might remain with her. Already the early splendor of the night was beginning to fade and although the moonlight still made the objects near by fairly distinct, farther off they were black and ghostlike. Perhaps for this reason Miss McMurtry at first made no sign, though believing she saw a small object dart forth from the shelter of the pine trees, run a few steps, crouch down and then getting up again run on a few feet more.

Of course she and the Camp Fire girls felt perfectly safe in their retreat in the woods, although just at the beginning of their encampment, when the nights closed down upon them, some few of the girls had felt awed and nervous, now after ten such experiences the sense of unfamiliarity was quite gone.

Sunrise Hill was on the border of the Webster farm, two miles from the village and well out of the way of trespassers. There were no wild animals about in these New Hampshire hills, for hunters had long since driven them away, and yet Miss McMurtry wondered dimly if the object plainly intending to come up to them could be an animal. She did not have to wonder very long, however, for the object soon rose on two legs and was plainly a human being.

What should be done? Miss McMurtry did not wish to alarm the younger girls, when there was no possible reason for fear, and yet she was annoyed, for if some one were trying to spy upon them at this hour the intruder must be summarily dealt with. Fortunately, Polly O'Neill had risen when her guardian did and happened to be standing next her at this minute. Slipping her arm through Polly's a slight movement drew her aside.

"Polly," she whispered, "there is something or someone coming toward us; let us go forward quietly and find out what or who it is."

Instantly catching the direction of Miss McMurtry's guarded glance, Polly, not hesitating a second, broke away and ran forward alone to meet the advancing figure. Nevertheless, the older woman followed so promptly that she was able to catch the girl's first words even before seeing the person to whom they were addressed.

"Why, Nan Graham, what do you mean by coming out here so late?" Polly demanded. "When I told you that you might look on at our Council Fire to-night I thought of course that you would come to camp before dark so that I could ask permission and explain."

Half leading, half pulling the newcomer, who after all was only another young girl, Polly drew her closer to the circle of their slowly dying fire. First she looked appealingly at their guardian, who had walked forward with them, and then from one of her friends' faces to the other until she found Betty's. There were no returning glances of sympathy from a single one of the Camp Fire girls.

Unfortunately, Nan Graham was not a stranger to any member of the Sunrise Hill club except to Juliet and Beatrice Field, who were themselves strangers in Woodford. Had Nan been, her reception would have been more cordial, even though appearing at night in so unconventional a fashion. But the newcomer had been a student with most of the girls at the high school the winter before and had been expelled for supposed dishonesty. Her family was impossible, the father, a man of good birth fallen so low that his own people would have nothing to do with him, had married an emigrant woman and Nan was one of many children. The girl had tried working in the village, but no one cared to trouble with her long. And yet she was just a little more than fifteen years old and not an unattractive looking girl, although her face was curiously older than any other girl's in the group about her. To-night she was wearing a shabby black frock, torn and dusty, and her coarse short black hair was unpleasantly disheveled.

"I couldn't leave home until late and then I lost my way," she replied finally, answering Polly's question in a sullen fashion because of the weight of disapproval.

"What right had you to say she could come, Polly O'Neill, when you understand that we like to keep our Council Fires to ourselves?" flashed Betty, and then stopped, knowing that it was plainly not her place to speak first.

"You should have returned home when you found you had mistaken the way," Miss McMurtry frowned. "You ought not to have come through the woods alone at this hour of the night, Nan, as you know perfectly well. But there is no way now for me to send you back to-night, though I am sure I don't know what to do with you. Polly, I think you owe it to us to explain why you invited a guest to camp and then gave us no warning so that we might have been prepared."

Under the influence of the meeting of the Council Fire and perhaps more under the spell of Polly's magnetism than she realized, Miss McMurtry, although it was plain that she was a good deal vexed, did not put her question severely.

So it was naturally irritating, not only to her but to a number of the girls as well, to have Polly, in the midst of the general disapproval, suddenly shrug her shoulders and give a characteristic laugh. "Oh, for goodness' sake, don't let us make a mountain out of a molehill!" she begged. "I was coming back to camp this afternoon and happening to pass Nan's home, she told me something that I thought it great fun for us to know. Some of our boy friends are coming out to camp to-morrow disguised as Indians and mean to take us by surprise. We can be prepared for them and so turn the joke around the other way. Well, after Nan told me this we talked for a little while, while Mollie and Bee and Sylvia walked on ahead. She seemed desperately anxious to hear about our camp and how we were living and what we were doing, so I told her to come along and see us. I really don't see that she can do us any harm. As far as to-night is concerned, why I will make up beds for us just outside our tent, for I have been wishing to sleep outdoors ever since we came into camp."

"And then I can go back home again in the morning," the newcomer said with a scowl. "I wasn't meaning to do any harm just by looking on."

Polly would have liked to have embraced Margaret Everett on the spot, for now separating herself from her friends she came shyly forward taking the strange girl's hand. "I am sorry you have had such a tiresome walk," she said kindly; "come let us all get ready for bed."

Mollie and Sylvia Wharton followed Meg's example in speaking to their unwelcome visitor, but Betty set the example for the others, by merely passing her by with a nod of her head.

However, when Esther and Mollie were both asleep, Betty came out from her tent and stood for a moment looking down at the two figures on their hastily improvised beds only a few feet away from her own tent.

One of them stirring, she bent over her whispering: "Good-night, Polly; of course there is no harm in Nan's being here one night, but please don't ask her to stay longer."

Margaret Vandercook

CHAPTER XIII

"NOBODY WANTS TO BE DONE GOOD TO"

A canoe containing three girls had been out on the waters of the lake near the foot of Sunrise Hill for the past two hours. A part of the time it had been swiftly shot through the water only to rest afterwards in certain shadowed places, where fishing lines were quietly dropped over its sides, until now a flat birch basket in its stern was filled with freshly caught fish.

There had been little conversation during this time, but now Polly O'Neill, letting her paddle rest for a moment, said to her fellow oarsman:

"Come, Betty, let us drift for a while. We don't have to get back to camp just yet, for it will be another two hours probably before our supposedly unexpected guests arrive, so we will have plenty of time to help with the preparations, to fry the fish and have Mollie make her inspired corn dodgers. It will be rather good fun when the Indian chiefs appear to strike terror to our hospitality, if not to our souls, for us to be ready and waiting for them, Semper paratus, always prepared, we can assure them is a Camp Fire girl's motto. But just now I wish to talk."

Betty's back was turned to the speaker, but her sister,

Mollie, sat facing her midway between the other two seats. Quietly and without replying Betty acquiesced in the request, permitting their canoe to glide slowly toward a small island and getting her kodak ready for action. One of her summer amusements was the making of a collection of animal and bird pictures, and now a large nest overhanging the water attracted her attention.

Therefore it was Mollie who replied to her sister, although the remark had not been made directly to her.

"Yes, Polly, we know you want to talk and we think we know what you want to talk about. I saw it on your face at breakfast even if Betty didn't and knew perfectly well why you persuaded Miss Martha to let us come with you for the fishing and no one else, even when Sylvia Wharton was almost in tears at being left behind."

"You don't know what I want to talk about, do you, Princess? Mollie is absurd, for I am sure I was not thinking of it at breakfast," Polly halloed, wishing that her friend's face was toward her so that she might gain something from her expression. A moment longer she had to wait for her answer because a great heron, startled by the noise, rose out of its nest flapping its great wings and ungainly legs and Betty's kodak instantly clicked with its appearance. Then she shook her head slowly, still not turning around, as she replied:

"Yes, I do know, Polly. That is why I would not agree to come with you until I had first had a little talk with Miss McMurtry. I didn't want to be obstinate if I am wrong, but she feels exactly as I do."

Polly whistled softly, two bright spots of color showing on her high cheek bones, a signal with her of being desperately in earnest. Nevertheless she returned indifferently: "Of course if Betty and our guardian agree, then have righteousness and truth met together and there is no use wasting my breath by putting in my poor little plea."

"There is no use in your being disagreeable, Polly," Mollie advised, who was not in the least afraid of scolding her sister, although rarely quarreling with her. "In this case I think Betty is entirely in the right, for this is not a question of money or family or many of the things you and Betty disagree about, it is a question of the person!"

"Gracious, what person?" Polly protested. "You are both talking riddles. Have I mentioned anybody's name or proposed any mortal thing? If I happen to be interested in this Nan Graham and to believe that things have been made pretty hard for her, is it anybody's business? I don't know just what it is about her that makes me feel as if she were a poor little hunted animal. I really don't think anybody has ever been even decently kind to her in her life; she has always had a bad name, and it must be a pretty hard thing to have to grow up in the shadow of one with no one to give you a boost. Take that affair at school; it was never positively proven that Nan was dishonest. Only she had told a few lies and her family was so horrid. Another girl might have been given another chance!"

"Well, we can't give her a chance at our Camp Fire club this summer, dear, Miss Martha is positive about it, so don't pretend that is not what you have on your mind," Betty interrupted. "I am sorry, but Miss Martha says she is a very different type of girl from the rest of us and might get us into trouble, and she is afraid our parents would not like her being with us."

"I don't know about parents, but I am sure mother wouldn't mind our helping another girl, perhaps just because she is different." And Polly's eyes filled with quick tears at the thought of her first long separation from her mother.

But Mollie shook her head slowly though not unsympathetically. "I am not so sure, Polly," she argued. "You know mother is always urging you to be sensible first and sentimental afterwards, and says that half the trouble in your life will come from working the other way round. Just take the question of the money; Nan Graham would never be able to pay her share, and although we let Mr. Ashton give us our camping outfit, each one of us is to pay her portion of our expenses and to try and find out how economical we can be. It isn't fair to impose a girl on Betty - "

"I have no idea of imposing Nan Graham on Betty," Polly interrupted hastily. "If it ever comes to be just a question of money, why I will promise to pay her expenses and to try to be responsible for her."

"You?" Mollie stared. "Polly O'Neill, you must be out of your senses. You know we have just barely enough for ourselves and are even trying to save a bit out of that, besides working at basket making and anything else we can do, to send mother some extra money."

Polly smiled in a superior fashion. "There are more ways for making money, Sinopa, than are dreamt of in your philosophy. I have my own reasons for not telling you, but I expect to come into a sum of money shortly which will certainly be more than enough to pay this poor Nan's expenses."

"But it is not the money that I care about in the least, Poay," Betty exclaimed, "and you know it! Somehow I am just afraid that in some way Nan will bring unhappiness among us."

"Of course it is not the money you care about, Princess." (Polly's apology was as ardent as her suggestion.) "Sometimes I wonder what would happen to you if you should ever be poor and have to learn to think about such an ugly, commonplace thing as money. Never mind, I am going to be an American Sarah Bernhardt and you and Mollie can travel about in my private car with me. But you understand if you agree to let Nan Graham stay in camp with us, I can't let her be an expense to you or the other girls."

By way of answer Betty looked at her watch. "It is getting pretty late, Polly, don't you think we had better get back to camp?" she proposed.

In perfect accord the two girls now swept their canoe back to their landing place, for they could row perfectly together, swim, paddle a canoe, ride, play tennis, in fact do everything except have the same opinions.

The two girls carried the basket of fish, leaving Mollie to tie up the canoe.

"I hope you don't feel very disappointed, Polly, it was because I was afraid you might think it a good idea to have Nan Graham join our Camp Fire club that I asked you not to think of it last night," Betty said, apologetically, sorry as always to disappoint her friend and not unaffected by her point of view.

"Ah, but you put it in my head, Betty Ashton. Really I never dreamed at first of letting Nan do anything more than come and see what our Camp Fire life was like. She was so eager and so interested when I met her yesterday that she seemed kind of pitiful to me. She told me she was dreadfully lonely because nice girls wouldn't have anything more to do with her now and yet she didn't want really to be bad. No one will take her to work, so she couldn't think what she could do with herself all summer. Last night when you went in to bed I kept on thinking about her and about what our Camp Fire may mean some day when we are older and stronger ourselves and understand more about it. Of course no one wants to be done good to, that is horrid and patronizing, but everybody wants to be made happier, rich people: and poor people too. Remember how you once said that Wohelo, Work, Health and. Love, solved all life's difficulties.

"Wohelo means love. We love Love, for love is life, and light and joy and sweetness, And love is comradeship and motherhood, and fatherhood, and all dear Kinship. Love is the joy of kinship so deep that self is forgotten."

"Now I wonder if comradeship and kinship really mean just caring about the people we would have had to care about anyway, our own friends or our own family?"

Having unconsciously touched upon one of the biggest questions in the world and having no answer, the two girls were both silent for a moment. Then Polly added in a surrender unusual to her:

"Don't worry, Betty, perhaps you are, right after all. Nobody can live up to all the things we preach. Anyhow it was, good of you to ask Miss Martha to let Nan spend the day with us. She says she will never get over the pleasure of it as long as she lives."

"Don't, Polly, really I do not think I can be expected to bear any more. You, have made me feel already that if Nan Graham ever does anything wrong or brings any sorrow on herself by her behavior, why it will somehow be my fault. Why do you make me responsible when you know Miss McMurtry and most of the other girls are just as opposed to having her with us as I am?" said Betty, realizing that her defense was a sign of weakness and yet feeling that Polly had somehow driven her to the wall.

"Because, Betty, you know that if you try you can bring some of the girls to your way of thinking and I can work on the others. Then together if we promise to be responsible for Nan's good behavior, why we may be able to influence Miss Martha."

Betty sighed. Mollie was catching up with them and they had almost reached camp, which was a scene of the most amazing activity.

"Ask me again to-night, Polly, I will try to think things over a little more."

There was no opportunity for any further discussion, for at this instant Meg and Eleanor swept down upon them.

CHAPTER XIV

SURPRISING THE CAMP

In the middle of the camping grounds on their return the girls now beheld Miss Martha McMurtry waving a large kitchen spoon in somewhat the same fashion that a conductor uses his baton to direct the energies of his orchestra. Rushing from one spot to the other her aides were engaged in putting fresh wood on one smoldering camp fire, stirring up slumbering ashes in another, removing kettles to different points of vantage and generally giving the impression that they were preparing for the feeding of an army. However, they were only getting ready for the entertainment of a few of their Boy Scout friends.

Early that morning Nan Graham had been made to explain more fully the information bestowed on Polly the day before. It seemed that her father had been engaged to do odd jobs at the camp of the Scouts several miles away from Sunrise Hill and had overheard the plan of the young men to test the mettle of the Camp Fire girls. Take them by surprise, bear down upon them without warning, that was the way to discover whether the girls were lolling about reading novels and eating sweets as they suspected, or attending to the sterner duties of camp life. Subject them to the trial of preparing an impromptu meal for hungry guests, in short, see whether the effort of the girls to effect an organization similar in many respects to the Boy Scouts wasn't sheer bluff.

Nothing had been said, because of course it must have been so easy to surmise the amount of criticism and discussion that arose in Woodford when the village learned of the decision of the first Camp Fire girls' club to spend the summer together in the woods. And sternest of all critics were the brothers, boy cousins and friends, most of whom belonged to the Boy Scout brigades, spending most of their spare time and money in them. For of course the thing that was good for a boy was for that very reason bad for a girl, an age old argument, beginning with the question of educating women at all and extending now to their right to the vote.

Curiously John Everett, Margaret's brother, was at first more bitterly opposed to the Camp Fire idea than any one else in Woodford. Meg's place was at home, every girl's was, even though there was no one at home with her. It was hard lines that his father had to be in Boston the greater part of the summer and that he would be in camp, but he was not going to have Meg getting drowned or burned up or worn out without masculine protection - away from home. Should any one of these misfortunes overtake her at home - why somehow it would be different.

But fortunately for Meg's summer happiness, her Professor father did not share in his son's opinions and after John had a long talk with Betty Ashton he became well, not convinced, but at least more open to conviction. Usually Betty did have this effect upon him, which was perhaps fortunate for them both.

So John Everett might certainly be expected as one of the surprise party and probably Jim Meade, Eleanor's brother Frank Wharton, and Ralph and Hugh Bowles, who belonged to the same group of friends, besides, well, it was the entire uncertainty in regard to the actual number of their visitors which was keeping the Camp Fire girls so extraordinarily busy, their idea being to have everything prepared and hidden away and then produced as though they were in the habit of having just such a magnificent supply of rations always on hand.

Eleanor and Meg had made an Irish stew of half their week's supply of meat and vegetables; Esther, assisted by Juliet Field, had baked enough beans for feeding half Beacon Street; while Miss McMurtry herself had presided over the giant loaves of brown bread, which can be easily boiled in closed tins and make specially superior camp food.

Upon Beatrice, Sylvia and the unwelcome newcomer, Nan Graham, had devolved the cleaning up of the camp grounds and their work had been most thoroughly done, but indeed no one could be accused, of anything approaching sloth this morning when so much of their future reputation was at stake. Only Edith Norton had been unable to help because of her work in town, but she hoped to be able to return to camp by noon so as not to miss the good times.

At eleven o'clock every bit of the work, of preparation had been accomplished and Nan's report had said that the Scouts expected to appear just about the noon luncheon hour. The food was hidden away in the kitchen tent and the girls rearranged their costumes, then after posting Nan, Beatrice and Sylvia as sentinels to give warning of the first approach of their guests, the other girls settled themselves to whatever occupations they considered might make the best impression.

Eleanor got out the Camp Fire log book, whose cover she had previously decorated with a wonderful sunrise appearing above the summit of a purple hill, and now began to illustrate some of the inside pages with scenes recalling the events of the past ten days. Mollie's tastes were too domestic for any deception, so she went on with her pretty basket weaving, while Esther sat near her studying the Indian song received the day before. However, the really impressive occupation was conceived and engineered by Polly's dramatic sense, for she engaged Miss McMurtry and the rest of the girls in the mysteries of knot tying, one of the difficult feats of camp craft, since there are a good many more varieties of knots than one has fingers. For example, there is the square knot, bowline, alpine, kite string, half hitch, clove hitch for tying two ends together, and as many more for making knots at the end of a rope, and yet, unless one happens to be a Camp Fire girl, these comparatively simple accomplishments are entirely closed arts.

Now everybody at Sunrise Camp is accounted for excepting its solitary masculine member - Little Brother. During all the morning preparations he had been a very difficult problem, but finally washed and arrayed in a stiff white Russian blouse, Meg conceived the brilliant idea of attaching him to the camp totem pole. The pole was simply a tree cleared of its branches at the present time, which the girls hoped later on to develop into a real Indian totem pole, but standing just a few yards in front of the group of tents it formed a center for all eyes and therefore seemed the best

Margaret Vandercook

possible place for keeping a little boy always in sight. Little Brother was at first very happy because he had with him the things he loved best: a discarded bathing shoe, a bottle of hard brown beans and an old cream whipper, that made the most delectable noises as one turned it about. Indeed, so soothing did its noises become that, on returning for the sixth time from her game to see that the small boy was safe, Meg discovered him fast asleep in a patch of sunshine on the grass.

Five minutes before noon Sylvia Wharton came running breathless with excitement from her sentry post. Dust was rising at some distance off in the curve of the lane where a path led across the fields to Sunrise Camp. Harder and faster the girls continued at their work, of course appearing superbly unconscious of possible interruption and yet ten minutes later, when Edith Norton returned from the village on her bicycle along the way of Sylvia's warning, there was a sort of general let-down feeling though no one confessed to it.

Then half an hour passed, noon was in the background of the day and hunger was laying fierce hold on the camp members. Their practice of knot tying abruptly ceased, Eleanor put her book and paints aside with a sense of relief, Mollie and Esther arose sighing.

"We have got to have our own lunch, girls, we simply can't wait any longer," Miss McMurtry insisted, and no one seemed sufficiently inspirited to discuss the question, when unexpectedly a cry from Meg brought everybody to life.

Little Brother had disappeared! In spite of the professional knot-tying he had managed to slip away, leaving his moorings still attached to the pole. Ten seconds afterwards as many girls were searching for him, only Esther remaining behind with Miss McMurtry. As his small footprints led directly to the grove of pines, his favorite playing ground, the entire party sought him there, and after running about for an eighth of a mile searching and calling, they came across the young man throned high on the shoulders of a six-foot Scout, clothed in khaki and leather boots but wearing a perfectly absurd Indian head-dress and false-face. He was followed by ten other youths, gotten up in equally absurd fashions for the complete bewilderment of the Camp Fire girls.

"Do take those ridiculous things off at once, John Everett," Betty demanded first, as she happened to be in advance of the other girls, and on John's immediately complying with her request, his companions followed his example. Then gaily the entire procession made for camp, but as Miss McMurtry and Esther heard them coming when some distance off, they did not seem particularly surprised at their advance. Indeed, the ridiculous fact was that the Scouts failed altogether to mention that their intention had been to steal into Sunrise Camp unperceived, and the girls were equally negligent in not expressing more profound amazement at their wholly unlooked-for visit.

Only there was one special bit of surprise for Betty Ashton and possibly for Esther as well. Richard Ashton had come down from Portsmouth to find out how Betty was getting on, and on hearing of the scouting expedition had joined their party. Of course he only spoke to Esther in the same fashion that he did to his sister's other friends, nevertheless she felt more at her ease, perhaps because he was her one acquaintance in the group of young men.

And Polly also had a surprise, though not so pleasant a one, for the youth whom she had tried to slay, like David did Goliath, was one of their Boy Scout guests and Polly wondered if it were her duty to inquire in regard to his wounded feelings or to pretend that to-day's more formal meeting was in reality their first?

CHAPTER XV

A WARNING

But the girl did not have to decide the problem, for the young man solved it for her.

They were in the midst of luncheon, which was spread out on a vast table-cloth covering ten or fifteen square feet of ground, when he arose solemnly and bearing his plate in his hand came over and sat down on the grass alongside of Polly. In his khaki uniform, with his hair, skin and clothes so much the same color, he was far less countrified, indeed, almost good looking the girl conceded to herself, while waiting for him to speak first, giving her the clue to his attitude toward her.

"You were awfully kind the other day and, I am much obliged to you," he said a trifle awkwardly, but with gracious intention. "I am afraid I should have had rather an uncomfortable time of it but for you."

Polly cast her eyes demurely toward her lap, turning her head slightly to one side, "I am afraid you did have an uncomfortable time anyhow. I was very sorry." She had flushed the least little bit, but her lips were twitching with amusement.

The young fellow smiled. "Oh, don't you be sorry," he

protested, "leave that to the guilty person, or I am afraid she may keep you being sorry for her sins all the days of your life."

"I will not!" Polly snapped, in such evident irritation that the young man leaned deliberately over her shoulder staring into her face. Then he actually laughed. "I am sorry myself now," he apologized, "but I thought you were the pretty one."

"Well I am not and that is a horrid way to get even!"

Again the young man laughed. "I beg your pardon, I mean I thought you were the nice one!" And this time Polly happening to catch his eye, which had some of her own sense of humor in it, laughed to herself and then swung round to talk to him more directly.

"No, I am neither the pretty one nor the nice one," she avowed. "There is Mollie sitting between Ralph Bowles and Frank Wharton and you can go talk to her in a moment. But just the same I am sorry that I happened to hit you the other day and I was just as much surprised at its having happened as you could possibly have been."

Her companion nodded as though to dismiss the subject. "If Mollie is the nice one and the pretty one, would you mind telling me your name, then perhaps next time I may be able to tell you apart without your giving me such strenuous examples of your differences in character. '

The girl shrugged her shoulders pretending to be entirely indifferent and yet a little piqued at the suggestion in the last sentence. The difference between herself and Mollie, all in her opinion in her sister's favor, was a sensitive subject.

"I was christened Pauline in baptism but I am usually known as Polly. However, my sister and I both recognize ourselves when called Miss O'Neill." This was such an evident attempt on Polly's part to put her questioner in his proper place that he could not rise entirely superior to it, even though her intention to hit back was so transparent.

"May I tell you my name now?" he asked in a more humble tone, as though wishful to make peace.

"You don't have to tell me your name for I am very sure I know it already," the girl answered in a provoking manner, for which she had a peculiar talent. "You see our guardian told us that you were the son of the Mr. Webster who owns the land on which we are camping, and I am convinced that there is no young man in New Hampshire boasting the last name, Webster, whose first name isn't Daniel! Do you think we would so fail to commemorate our greatest statesman? It must be rather dreary to be named for so great a person that you know whatever you may achieve yourself you must always sound like an anti-climax."

This time it was surely Polly who had struck home, for the young man colored and applied himself to the food on his plate for at least a moment before he replied: "You are right, my name is Daniel and I have felt about it a little as you say, but then I am also called William, which is a better name for a farmer."

"Farmer?" Polly forgot that she and her companion had

been sparring and let a genuine interest creep into her tone. "Do you really mean that you are going to be content to be a farmer all the days of your life, to stay right on here and never see anything or be anything else? It sounds so strange to me - for a man to have no ambition! ' Almost she forgot her companion and sat frowning with her eyes more serious than usual and her thin face with its sensitive features and high cheek bones turned upward toward the peak of Sunrise Hill. "I am a girl, but I am going all over the world and I am going to be an actress and do ten thousand delightful things just as fast as I can before I have a chance to get old."

Gazing at her more intently than ever before in their conversation, the young fellow shook his head. "No you won't,"' he said bluntly, "you will never be strong enough and you had better stay here in the hills and let some one look after you, your sister or - some one. Yet you need not talk as though being a farmer was a thing to look down upon. I am sure our great men all used to be farmers, George Washington and the rest of 'em. You must know their names better than I do. So please bear in mind that I intend to do my best to make things grow - hayseed!" he laughed good humouredly, guessing Polly's secret scorn of him, "but at the same time I expect to see something and if I'm lucky to be something, though if I'm a first-class farmer it isn't so worse. Do give me your plate, you have eaten very little and the rest of the crowd is getting dreadfully ahead of us "

But Polly, jumping up hastily and the young man following her, led him over and introduced him to Mollie, with whom he spent the greater part of the afternoon.

From two o'clock till sundown the hours at Sunrise, Camp were fairly strenuous ones since the Camp Fire girls insisted on comparative tests of skill with their Boy Scout guests. Of course the young men agreed, although they were pleasantly scornful, until possibly owing to their morning's contest the girls actually won out in the knot-tying contest, which was supposed to be a peculiarly masculine accomplishment. In running, jumping and feats of marksmanship the girls of course were easily outclassed by their opponents; however, Beatrice Field, who was so light and so small that no one considered her in the race, did come in second in a short thirty-yard dash. Then Miss McMurtry held a kind of impromptu examination in questions of patriotism and nature lore, the girls and men managing to about equally divide the honors. But the really extra-ordinary feature of the afternoon was that dull little Sylvia Wharton, the youngest member of the company, was easily first in half a dozen observation games most important in the training of Camp Fire girls and Boy Scouts. For instance, in a Quick-sight experiment, the girls and boys walking rapidly from the camping ground to the shores of the lake, Sylvia had seen eight small objects more than any one else and she was so quiet and looked so stolid while doing it that Polly wanted to laugh, and began to doubt her stupidity.

At six o'clock it still appeared as though the Boy Scouts intended remaining for the evening meal and camp fire; however, Miss McMurtry kindly but firmly bade them farewell. The girls were tired and it was a long tramp back to the Scout camp. There had been no suggestion from any one that the surprise visit had been made in any spirit of criticism and yet John Everett made a half-hearted apology to Betty and his sister.

When the farewells were being said all round, he called the two girls aside:

"I say," he murmured boyishly, in spite of his years and six feet, "I have got to confess that I never saw you girls looking so well, so kind of up to the limit before, and I thought by this time you would surely be fagged out, or bored, or sick of trying things out together. Now I don t say I approve of this Camp Fire business, I won't go so far as that, but it does not seem to have done either of you any harm yet."

And then laughing at his grudging attitude the three of them rejoined their friends, who were waiting to end their day together by singing "My Country, 'Tis of Thee." And they were waiting because Esther Clark was needed for leading the song and in the last few moments she had disappeared with Richard Ashton, who had been watching the proceedings all day with an expression that was sometimes amused but the greater part of the time grave. He had no opportunity for speaking to Betty or to any one else alone and only to Esther because he had just made a deliberate effort. As they came slowly back from the pine grove together, Betty felt cross at Dick's choice of a companion when any one of her other friends would have been pleased by his attention.

Then, too, Esther looked as serious as her brother and Betty hated unnecessary seriousness, besides Dick needed some one to make him gay, not an awkward, uninteresting acquaintance like Esther. But there was no use in arguing with Dick, for he would always be kind to the people who were left out of things and seemed most to require kindness. Sorry to have seen so little of her brother during his short visit, Betty now slipped her hand into his and held it tight while Esther, standing some distance apart from them, started the air for their parting hymn. The girl was not thinking of herself and so was unconscious that the others, even while singing, were also listening with surprise and pleasure to the clear, rounded tones of her beautiful mezzo-soprano voice. In reality Esther Clark was thinking only of Betty and the news that Dick Ashton had just told her. Mr. Ashton, his father, had been taken ill in Italy and, though there was no immediate danger, might never be well again. For the present it was thought best that he remain indefinitely in Europe, so the family had not decided whether or not to tell the facts to Betty. She could do no good; even Dick was not going to him, and it was always best to keep every possible sorrow from Betty. But really, because Dick Ashton could not make up his mind just what was the wisest course, he confided his secret to Esther, asking her to think matters over and write him her judgment. You see there was no question of Esther's unusual devotion to Betty and readiness to sacrifice everything for her, though there seemed to be no reason, and surely Betty was entirely careless of it.

Before the twilight of the long afternoon had entirely faded into night, every Camp Fire girl, including Nan Graham, who was not a member, had vanished into bed. The child was too tired to be sent home to-night and word would be taken to her parents by one of the boys. Miss McMurtry herself was asleep as soon as her girls. And indeed Polly entirely forgot that Betty had suggested she put the question of Nan's remaining in camp with them to her again during the evening.

How many hours Polly had been asleep outside her

tent with the newcomer by her side she did not know, but suddenly she was awakened by a sound that was like a sob. Sitting up quickly she saw Nan kneeling on the ground and looking up at the sky.

Polly waited in silence until the girl, feeling her wakefulness, came slowly back to her own bed and somehow Polly could see that her face had lost its sharp, old look and was like a child's.

"I was praying you'd keep me in camp with you long enough to give me a try," she explained.

Like a flash Betty's suggestion that she might change her opinion after thinking things over came back to Polly's mind. Of course the day had not been conducive to reflection, but perhaps it might be just as well not to give Betty too much time to think.

Half an hour afterwards Polly crawled under the blue blankets and putting her arms about her friend whispered her request. And just at first Betty was too sleepy to know what was being asked of her and later on was possibly too tired to resist, for she yawned an agreement.

"Oh yes, I will do my best to persuade the girls to let her stay on if you want her and Miss Martha consents. But if there is trouble, Polly - " and she was almost asleep again.

Polly gave her another gentle shake. "Promise to keep your money hidden and not put temptation in her way. Esther says she found your pocketbook stuffed with money in the middle of the tent floor."

"I promise," Betty ended hardly knowing what she said.

Margaret Vandercook

CHAPTER XVI

LEARNING TO KEEP STEP

Six weeks had passed by and it was now early August in the New Hampshire hills. Six wonderful weeks for the Camp Fire girls at Sunrise Hill, moving so swiftly that it seemed almost incredible so much time could have gone by. Everybody had kept well, nothing had ruffled their harmonies, except occasional differences of opinion which were easily adjusted, and yet Nan Graham had continued a member of the camp.

By this time the new influences in many ways showed their effect upon her. At first she was inclined to use language that shocked and annoyed both the girls and their guardian. She was not lazy and yet regular hours for work seemed irksome to her; she wanted to work when it was play time and play when work should be accomplished, and then her personal habits were not pleasant; but this was because she had never been taught better, for very soon she grew to be as neat as any of her companions and though her clothes were worn and shabby they were carefully washed twice a week by her own hands because she had fewer possessions than the other girls. In the beginning Betty had given her several blouses and some underclothes and would have done far more except that Miss McMurtry advised her to cease. For it was not fair that

Nan should not also learn a spirit of independence and the desire to earn her own way. Miss McMurtry hoped that the Camp Fire might teach the girls this as one of its best lessons. Always we have believed that the American boy can make his own place in the world, given an education and a healthy body, then why not the American girl as well, now that she is to have almost the same opportunity and encouragement?

Notwithstanding that, there was one serious, indeed most serious, fault that the new Camp Fire member had not yet man aged to overcome: she was not always truthful. The stories she told did not appear to be malicious or very important, they merely explained why she was late when her hour came for work, how she had gained certain elective honors when no one was by to witness them, and yet they caused a general feeling of distrust when evidence upon a question depended solely on Nan's word. Miss McMurtry had talked to her many times and always she had promised never to offend again and yet a habit of untruthfulness is not so easily conquered. In reality, Polly O'Neill had more influence with the girl whose cause she had championed than anyone else in camp, so that once or twice Miss Martha had been tempted to ask Polly to talk to her and then had given up the idea, thinking that perhaps it was hardly fair for one girl to be told to lecture another.

However, it was surprising to see how kind and sympathetic the little group of Camp Fire members tried to be to their least fortunate member and up to the present time Miss McMurtry felt glad that she had yielded her first judgment in the matter and allowed Nan to stay on with them. Even Betty, although unable to be intimate with a girl whose family connections and manners so tried her aristocratic soul, was always considerate and certainly at the end of each week it had been Betty who had quietly paid Nan's share of their expenses without a word. That there had ever been a question of any one else's doing it, no one except Betty, Polly and Mollie knew. And just what Polly had suffered at the end of each week when she had failed to fulfill her contract no one except a girl with exactly her disposition can understand. For the money which she had spoken of so mysteriously to her sister and friend had up till now failed to materialize. Nevertheless Polly had not lost hope, but several times had assured Betty that she would pay her the entire amount advanced for Nan almost any day, and the very fact that Betty begged her not to think of this made her the more insistent.

Thirteen was Polly O'Neill's lucky number. Possibly because it was regarded as an unlucky figure by other people Polly had selected and cherished it for her own, and with the Irish ability to prove things, because one wishes them to be true, she could give a long list of happy events in her past history all taking place on the thirteenth day of the mouth. Besides, had she and Molly not been born on the thirteenth, naturally fitting the date to her star?

So on the thirteenth of August (although no one else in camp happened to have thought of that day of the month) Polly begged leave of their guardian to go alone into Woodford on a most important errand. The girls were not in the habit of going into town alone; perhaps because the walk was a long one no one had ever wished before to go without company. However, there was no conspicuous objection since the way led through the Webster farm and then on to the high road into the village, and, moreover, Polly insisted that her reason for wishing to go unaccompanied was a highly important one.

Nevertheless, with a slight feeling of discomfort, Miss McMurtry saw her start off after lunch. Though the subject was not discussed she realized that Polly O'Neill was physically less strong than most girls and that her high spirits and nervous energy often gave a wrong impression.

To-day, however, Polly seemed particularly well and curiously eager, so that the other girls teased her all through luncheon endeavoring to find out the cause of her mysterious errand, without gaining the least clue. Betty and Mollie were both offended by her secrecy in spite of her promise to tell them everything should matters turn out as she expected.

Polly believed in destiny, or at least in her own destiny as we all should, but now and then, fear taking possession, her faith was less secure.

There had been a few of these hours in the past six weeks while she had prayed, hoped and willed one thing, but almost always she had believed in it with her whole heart. Waking at daylight on this morning of the thirteenth of August and seeing a particularly wonderful sunrise, a curious wave of conviction had swept over her. To-day she would see her desire fulfilled!

Truly the day was a beautiful one, a day for all lovely dreams to come true, and as Polly walked through the fields, heavy and golden with the ripened grain, the Irish buoyancy of her temperament asserting itself, made each object appear an omen of good luck - the sight of a bluebird meant happiness of course, the flight of a carrier pigeon the arrival of a longed-for message. Weary finally of thinking delightful things Polly fell to reciting poetry aloud. As a small girl and in spite of her mother's and sister's protests she had made up her mind to be an actress and had devoted all her spare hours to the memorizing of poetry and plays. Therefore there were many hours when she loved dearly to be alone just in order to repeat some of the lines over and over, trying to read into them their deeper meaning, without an audience to be either bored or amused.

Particularly had she loved and learned the strange, musical Irish poetry of William Butler Yeats. Perhaps because the Irish believed in fairies Polly did too, although she called her fairies by other names.

Now all alone in the yellow fields she recited the closing lines of "The Land of Heart's Desire," doing her level best to put into it some little portion of its mystical beauty. She was not altogether successful because she was only a girl without any training or knowledge of her art, but perhaps because of her youth she was less afraid and filled with a sincerer enthusiasm.

"The wind blows out of the gates of the day, The wind blows over the lonely of heart, And the lonely of heart is withered away While the faeries dance in a place apart, Shaking their milk-white feet in a ring, Tossing their milk-white arms in the air; For they hear the wind laugh and murmur and sing Of a land where even the old are fair, And even the wise are merry of tongue; But I heard a reed of Coolaney say, When the wind has laughed and murmured and sung, The lonely of heart is withered away."

And then, after having repeated her verse three times and feeling that she was no nearer than at first to expressing its beauty, Polly found herself through the fields and after passing by a small stretch of woodlands would be out on the high road and therefore no longer alone.

And here, just at the entrance to the woodland, Polly's foot struck against something, and stooping over she picked up from the ground the answer to her desire, not the expected answer but one that would do as well in its stead.

Naturally she forgot to be reasonable or sensible, forgot everything save the good luck that seemed to come as an answer to prayer.

At the village post-office she did not even think to ask for her mail, although stopping long enough to write a short letter to her mother, enclosing a portion of her discovery and asking that it be used to purchase a present for the new English cousin about whom her mother had lately written so much.

Neither was there a confession made either to Mollie or Betty or any one else at camp that evening, since it was far pleasanter to appear cloaked in mystery; but Polly secured peace for herself by bringing back with her a large basket of peaches to glorify their supper party, and then later that evening quietly presented Betty with the amount in full advanced for Nan Graham's expenses. She said nothing about the way in which the money had been obtained and although

Betty was curious to know, good taste forbade her asking questions.

CHAPTER XVII

THE SUSPICION

Miss McMurtry and Betty had been alone together in one of the tents for the past half hour. Not that this was in any way remarkable or at first excited any suspicion, for the young woman and girl had become good friends in the past weeks, often consulting with one another concerning questions of camp life. Indeed Betty had been chiefly responsible for bestowing on their guardian her pretty new title, although the name had really developed from the suggestion first made by Mollie O'Neill and later turned into a jest by her sister.

"Our Lady of the Hill" was now Miss McMurtry's title as guardian of the Sunrise Camp. But because the expression was too long a one for ordinary conversation, "Donna," the soft Italian word for "lady," was more often substituted.

"I don't think I can be mistaken, Donna," Betty now returned seriously, her face flushed and her gray eyes unusually grave. "I don't want you to think I would make trouble in camp for all the world, as it is all probably my fault, but Esther was with me and has the same impression I have. She thought I ought to speak to you as a kind of warning to the other girls. I wish you would let me call Esther."

Miss McMurtry agreed, frowning uncomfortably and resting her head on one hand. Since outdoor life gives one whatever help is needed, she had grown far less thin with her months of fresh air, her figure was less angular, her expression less learned and her whole manner more like a girl's than an old maid's. Possibly the gracious dignity of her new title was also worth living up to.

"I must not be in too much of a hurry or too severe," she afterwards murmured to herself, "but from the first I have been dreadfully afraid of something like this."

Esther was discovered sitting with the other girls in a group surrounding Polly, who had been reading aloud an old folk tale while the others worked at their various hand crafts. Betty apologized for the interruption in leaning over to whisper to Esther, but half guessed at Polly's irritation as they hurried off together. However, if it could be prevented, Polly was to hear of their trouble last of all!

And Polly, although not acknowledging it, was annoyed, for lately Betty and Esther had seemed more intimate than she could ever have dreamed they might be. Not that Betty appeared to feel any affection for the older girl, but having heard through her of her father's illness they had been drawn together by Esther's constant sympathy and devotion, and although Mr. Ashton was now better Betty had not yet forgotten. Of course Polly was not jealous, that would be too small minded and absurd, only it was curious for her dearest friend to be sharing her secrets with other persons than herself.

Inside the tent with their guardian, Esther was being

more explicit in her explanation than Betty had been.

"You see," she said, "I understand better about temptations of that kind than Betty, because I have been brought up so differently, so when the letter came I begged her to be particularly careful, and we hid it together in a small lock-box in our tent. The strange thing is that the letter is still there and the outside envelope, but the envelope in which the package was enclosed I found crumpled up near Nan's cot when I was cleaning this morning."

Miss McMurtry shook her head more cheerfully. "That isn't enough evidence, children, to use against any human being! And just because this poor Nan has one story against her, don't you think we ought to be especially careful about adding another?"

Instead of replying at once Betty looked more miserable instead of less, and then biting her lips for an instant answered steadily:

"Yes, you are quite right, Donna, and we won't say another word about the loss. I am sorry and I confess a little disappointed, for father wished us to have a party in honor of his being better, but the party couldn't make us nearly as happy as this story would make us unhappy once we allowed it to be told."

Miss McMurtry caught Betty's hand and kissed it unexpectedly. Betty was spoiled, accepting love and good fortune too much as a matter of course, but when it came to a question either of generosity or good breeding Betty Ashton could always be counted upon.

However, Esther Clark was not so persuaded. "I am

afraid Betty may be angry with me and that you will be more uncomfortable, Miss McMurtry," she added after a moment's hesitation. "But this is not all the evidence we have. You see Mollie told us yesterday that just the next day after we girls made our trip to town and returned with the mail, she came across Nan in our tent with Betty's bunch of keys in her hand. It is true that Betty had left her keys out on the table, but I don't see what Nan could have wanted with them?"

"She told Mollie that she wanted to peep in my trunk to look at a dress I have because she wanted some day to make herself one like it and did not know just how," Betty interposed, using no effort to hide the tears that had been gathering in her gray eyes and were now coursing down her cheeks. "Oh dear me, I do wish I had not brought the wretched money into camp, for I promised Polly I would not put temptation in Nan's way and she will be dreadfully cross with me if she hears!"

"I don't think you should blame yourself, dear," Miss McMurtry interrupted, drawing Betty closer to her and looking almost ready to cry herself as they both turned toward Esther for advice. For somehow Esther might have a shy and awkward personality and not seem of much importance when things were going happily, yet in sorrow or difficulty, insensibly her gravity and unselfishness counted.

"Don't you think we had better send for Nan and let her offer us some explanation," Esther unhesitatingly suggested, "perhaps she will be able to make everything clear?"

Miss McMurtry and, Betty were both silent and Betty

moved quietly toward the opening of the tent. "You really will have to let me go away," she pleaded, "for I can't stand up and accuse one of our own Camp Fire girls of having - " Her sentence remained unfinished, but Miss McMurtry was able to catch hold of her skirt. "You can't leave us in the lurch, Betty, child, though I do understand your feelings, you must stand by to help Esther and me out. Certainly we shall not accuse poor Nan of anything, merely ask her a question. Esther, will you find her for us?"

Betty smiled tearfully as Esther went away on the errand, wondering if this time Miss Martha feared to trust her.

Ten minutes passed and then fifteen and yet neither Esther nor Nan appeared. Finally, however, Esther returned looking unusually angry and crestfallen. "Nan says she won't come until Polly has finished the story she is reading, and that probably may take another half hour," she reported. "I told her that you wished her particularly, Miss McMurtry, and waited as long as I could, but she showed no sign of obeying."

"That isn't true, or at least it is only half true, which is as bad," a voice declared at this instant at Esther's elbow, and Nan Graham pushed her way saucily into the tent, rather pleased at making serious Esther flush with displeasure. But at the sight of Betty, whom she always admired, and their guardian, whom she a little feared, her expression became less bold and, indeed, before any one spoke the girl's face had a strange look of guilt. Why else should she toss her head and bridle so unnecessarily, why stare into Miss McMurtry's eyes with her own hard and defiant, even while her lips trembled with nervousness?

"I haven't done anything; what do you want with me?" she asked quickly.

"No, Nan, we only want to ask you a question," Miss McMurtry answered, speaking as gently as she knew how. "Would you mind telling us what you were doing with Betty Ashton's keys the other afternoon and how you happened to get hold of them?"

"I didn't have her keys, that's a lie," Nan returned fiercely, taken off her guard and using a word she had always been accustomed to hear in her home.

To save the situation Betty came quickly forward. "Please don't say that, Nan," she begged, "for Mollie has already told us you merely wanted to look at my blue dress and that was quite all right. But if you deny it, why - "

"Why what?" Nan demanded sullenly, her black eyes on the ground and her face, which had turned a healthier color with her weeks in the woods, now white and drawn.

"Why we might not believe you when asking a more important question," Miss McMurtry said sternly, angered in spite of herself by the girl's disagreeable manner. "How many times have I told you that when people are untruthful about little things one does not believe them in large. The fact is that Betty has lost a large sum of money and - "

"And you believe I stole it!" Nan burst into such a violent storm of weeping at this suggestion that Betty for the first time in their acquaintance actually put her arm about her.

"No, we don't believe you took it just because it has vanished," she whispered comfortingly, casting appealing glances at her guardian and Esther, "only we want to ask you to try to help us find out about it. I wouldn't be in the least surprised if it should turn up again!"

Neither Miss McMurtry nor Esther spoke, but Nan was not to be so appeased.

"I am sure you are very kind to give me this opportunity to put your old money back," she answered bitterly, "but as I did not take it I should find that pretty difficult. I didn't even know you had any money, although I confess I did look into your trunk when perhaps I ought to have asked permission and I did take out an old blouse, but I was sorry the next minute and put it back again. But I expect I might as well have kept it and anything else I could lay my hands on. It is the old story, if a girl does a wrong thing once no one ever believes in her when she tries to be straight again. I suppose you will be telling your suspicion to Polly O'Neill and the other girls so they won't let me stay any longer in camp. I don't care, I am innocent!" Nan's voice rose to a shrill cry of protest, but in spite of this there was a note of sincerity in it that almost convinced Betty, although unfortunately the effect was not the same upon Miss McMurtry and Esther.

"No one shall say anything against you, Nan, nor spread this story in any possible way until more is found out," Miss McMurtry now remarked, briefly dismissing them.

CHAPTER XVIII

ONE WAY TO FIND OUT

Nevertheless within a few days the story had been circulated about the camp. Not a word, however, had been spoken concerning it by Betty, Esther or Miss McMurtry, but poor Nan Graham had betrayed herself. For in her effort to gain sympathizers, unfortunately a wider suspicion was aroused.

Sore and unhappy over what she insisted was a totally unjust supposition, it was but natural that she should turn to another girl for consolation. Not to Polly, however; Nan said not a word to her, for Polly had given no evidence of having heard of her ill-timed visit to Betty's trunk, having been on her way to the village at the time the offence was committed, and above everything Nan desired to remain fixed in Polly's good graces. No, she confided the account of her interview first to Beatrice Field, making so tragic a tale of it that Bee, who was quite young and only a mischievous tomboy in her disposition and never having heard anything of Nan's past mistakes, was deeply indignant.

"A Camp Fire girl accused of stealing, well not exactly accused but suspected!" Honestly Bee had never conceived of anything so dreadful, and so straightway put the whole case before her sister, Juliet. Then to her surprise Juliet, who was a far more worldly wise person, did not accept the story from the same point of view, indeed Juliet became immediately indignant for Betty's sake, declaring that she was being a martyr in not spreading the news of her loss abroad and at least endeavoring to recover her lost property.

Something of Juliet's impression must have crept into Bee, for in her next conversation with Nan there was a certain cooling off in sympathy that made Nan feel the need of another partisan. This time she was more unwise in selecting Edith Norton, for Edith had always particularly disliked Nan's presence in the Sunrise Camp and, even while hearing her side of the story, had unhesitatingly revealed not only a want of pity for her but a plain lack of faith.

Nan had forgotten to require at the beginning of their conversation that Edith keep her confidence a secret and so the older girl made no pretence of doing so. In her bitterness Nan had not hesitated to say hard things of Betty, Esther and even of their guardian in speaking of the injustice of their attitude toward her, and these remarks Edith felt free to add to her own account. Not that she really meant to be cruel or unfair, but honestly feeling it best that Nan stay no longer in their camp she started a campaign toward that end. Perhaps because Edith was poor and self-supporting herself, unconsciously she resented the presence of another girl whose poverty was of so much less honorable a kind, for it is more difficult to be fair to persons almost in our own state of life than to those in far different ones.

Not long did Edith remain alone in her conviction, for the layer of real faith and affection for poor little Nan in camp was so thin that the first effort broke through it. In point of fact no one had actually wanted her at Sunrise Camp and had only been persuaded into it by Polly and Betty and by Miss McMurtry's approval, and really these three persons were still the only three who continued her champions.

Betty would not hear for an instant of Nan's being sent away, threatened to leave herself rather than be responsible for such an act of injustice. Miss McMurtry was equally firm, although she added that Nan was not to be condemned until further proof was secured against her. Meanwhile Polly O'Neill was really unaware for some time of the actual circumstances of the case. In the first place Betty had begged that the story be kept from Polly as Nan was her especial protegee, and seeing what a storm had been aroused in camp she herself felt more than sorry ever to have mentioned her loss. Of course Polly heard vaguely that Betty had lost something or other about camp, but she did not know exactly what, but then Betty had so many possessions that she was always losing something. Also she began to suspect, dimly at first, that the girls were in some kind of quandary, but as no one mentioned the cause to her, she felt rather too proud to inquire, besides having a problem of her own on her mind which taxed most of her waking hours, although she too kept her own counsel.

But now a sufficient time had gone by, until the date of the meeting of the August Council Fire had arrived when the original number of Camp Fire members were to be promoted to the rank of Fire-Makers and Esther was to be first of the Sunrise Hill girls to be given the highest Camp Fire title - Torch Bearer.

One of Miss McMurtry's plans for her camp was to

leave to three girls each month the arrangements for the original features of their Council Fire and in August, the month of the Red or Green Corn Moon, it so happened that Mollie, Eleanor and Edith Norton formed the special committee. Just what their plans were no one knew until the morning before their meeting, not even the camp guardian, or Miss McMurtry might possibly have interfered, although I hardly believe it.

Shortly after breakfast, even before the other girls had a chance to disperse for their morning's work, Eleanor, Mollie and Edith Norton disappeared inside their tents.

Edith had been chosen to help at this meeting rather than any other because she was now having her two weeks' August vacation. Ten minutes later the girls came out again into the open air, arrayed in their ceremonial costumes and carrying three Indian baskets which were solemnly passed about from one girl to the other. And these baskets contained invitations to the evening Council Fire painted on bits of birch bark in crimson lettering by Eleanor Meade.

At the top of the scroll were the three words "The Maidens' Feast." Then below, the invitation read: "Sinopa the Little Sister, Apoi-a-kimi, the Light Hair, and Eleanor, the Painter of Sunrises, invite all the maidens of all the tribes to come and partake of their feast this evening at the close of the regular Council Fire ceremonies. It will be in the Sunrise Camp before the moon reaches the middle sky. All pure maidens are invited."

CHAPTER XIX

THE DISAPPEARANCE

The August moon had never been more radiant, indeed it flooded the Sunrise Camp grounds with a brightness that made it appear almost like day. And now the regular Council Fire proceedings were over and the Indian custom of "The Maidens' Feast" about to begin.

In a circle about a cone-shaped rock, which had been brought with infinite difficulty to its position in the camp grounds, Miss McMurtry and the maidens were seated, each person bearing in her lap a round wooden bowl, while from the smoldering ashes of the Council Fire arose a delicious odor of roasting ears of corn.

But before the feast could be eaten a ceremony of as grave importance to the Camp Fire girls as to the Indian maidens of long ago must take place. Each girl was to take the oath of purity and honor, and then the maidens' song would be sung and four times they would dance around the altar.

No one of the group of Camp Fire members and no more their guardian really knew at first whether in this plan of Eleanor's, Mollie's and Edith's there was any deeper motive than the entertainment of their friends and the revival of an old Indian custom seemingly appropriate and beautiful. But as the details unfolded themselves the suspicion in the minds of most of them grew almost into certainty. Once or twice Miss McMurtry had thought of stopping the proceedings altogether, but then she did not feel satisfied that this method of the three girls for testing the innocence or guilt of their companions was not an admirable one. More than she would have acknowledged, since worry is not permitted in Camp Fire rules, had Miss McMurtry puzzled over what should be done in their present dilemma. Betty's money had certainly disappeared and some one must have stolen it; if not Nan, then who else? For they had had no guests since Esther and Betty returned with the money from the village post-office.

So by the time Edith Norton, with her light hair hanging loose about her shoulders and a circle of red about her head, stepped forth into the center of the circle, looking unusually white and nervous, there was not but one member of her audience who did not at least partially guess at what was about to take place. And this was of course Polly O'Neill! For not only did she fail to understand Betty's actual money loss and the suspicion against Nan, but so deeply had she been involved in her own perplexity that she had hardly been aware of anything that had taken place that evening. Now, however, having at last made up her mind to take Miss McMurtry into her confidence when the girls had gone to bed, she did look up with interest at the picturesque figure of Edith.

Near the cone-shaped rock two arrows had been lightly stuck into the ground, this forming a sort of altar to which each maiden must come, touching first the stone and then the arrows as she declares her purity.

As she stood by the side of this altar Edith's voice trembled so that it was with difficulty her first words could be understood. The girls who knew pretty well what to expect understood her immediately, however, but not Polly!

"Sorrow and much uneasiness have lately crept into our midst, my maidens," she announced, trying to preserve a certain likeness to the Indian speech in the form of her words, "and many of us there are who go about heavy of heart because the sin of one of us must be the burden of us all, until guilt is established and the innocent cleared. Some days ago there vanished from the possession of one of us fifty dollars in bank notes enclosed in an envelope containing no address. This money has not been found, but the envelope has been recognized as crumpled up and thrown away a few feet from the tent of its rightful owner. Now no member of the Sunrise Camp can feel it possible that any one of its members has been guilty of this sin and yet no visitor has stepped foot within our camp limits within the time when the deed must have occurred. Therefore have we three maidens, after deep thought, appointed this evening wherein the innocent may declare her innocence and the wrong-doer confess her sin. For only in confession and by the return of the money can she ever hope to be at peace with herself. Moreover, we believe that no Camp Fire girl will take this oath of purity without telling the entire truth. Betty Ashton will you come forward first."

Betty jumped up quickly. During Edith's long harangue her group of listeners had been supremely uncomfortable, so that no one of them dared do more than barely glance at Nan, who sat with her knees up to her chin, her eyes cast upon the ground and her black hair covering her face like a veil. If she felt, and of course she did, that Edith's speech was directed toward her rather than toward any other girl, neither by a sound nor a movement did she betray it. Not even when Betty, having finished with her part in the ceremony, deliberately forsaking her former place in the circle came back and sitting down next her deliberately laid her arm across Nan's bowed shoulders. There was nothing to do or say, she would only make things worse by any protest now, and yet Betty was bitterly grieved and offended. If Nan had done wrong this public method of making her either confess or perjure herself she felt to be wholly unkind.

So as Nan was in everybody's thoughts during this time no one happened to glance toward Polly O'Neill or, seeing her, to observe anything unusual in her manner or appearance, for Polly also neither moved nor spoke during Edith's recital, although her face turned suddenly white.

Fifty dollars in an envelope, the money in bank notes and the envelope crumpled up and thrown away near their tent! Her discovery in the woods that day had been just this and she herself had thrown away that same envelope. Betty of course had lost the enclosure out of her letter in bringing it home from the post office and, hiding the letter away afterwards, believed the money still there.

Why did not Polly get up and make this announcement at once? It would have been very simple except for one thing, she had spent the money, and in the first moment of surprised horror had no idea how she would ever be able to return it.

Like a good many impetuous people Polly O'Neill sometimes had the misfortune to do her thinking when it was too late. Finding the money in the woods, when she felt she needed it so much, had seemed to her like a miracle, so that it never occurred to her, either that afternoon or evening, that she should have tried to find out to whom the money rightfully belonged before using it, although she had been thinking of little else since then. That this money should have been Betty's of all people, and that it was now her duty to stand up and confess her mistake before her friends.

Polly set her teeth, the circle of girls revolved before her eyes, she had been worrying too much to be either reasonable or well. And at any moment Edith Norton might demand that she step forward and take the oath which was meant to proclaim that she had had nothing to do with the loss of Betty's money. Truly she did not understand that the charge had been directed against poor Nan, so watching her opportunity Polly slipped away without being noticed.

When Nan Graham's name was called from the center of the circle the silence was oppressive. But the girl rose up quietly, pushing her coarse black hair from her face, and as quietly walked forward to the cone-shaped rock where the two arrows were still standing fixed in the ground. Before laying her hand on these objects, however, she stood perfectly still for a moment, letting her accusing eyes sweep from the face of one of her girl judges to the other and then, touching the stone and the arrows, came back quickly to her old place. Not till then did she betray how deeply the atmosphere of distrust and unfaith had hurt her, but when Betty's arm came round her for the second time, she burst into weeping, hiding her face on Betty's shoulder, and hearing her whisper comfortingly: "I believe with all my heart that you know nothing of my wretched money, Nan, and I beg your pardon if I even made you think I suspected you."

Just before the time for Polly to take the oath her absence was discovered, but not until the feast of the corn had actually begun did Mollie and Betty go back to their tent to look for her and they did not return for so long a time that Miss McMurtry, fearing Polly might be ill, rose up to follow them. However, she had only gone a few steps before the two girls joined her.

"We can't find Polly anywhere, Donna," Mollie said in an extremely annoyed tone. "We have looked in all the tents and called and even gone down to the pine grove. What silly mood do you suppose has overtaken her? For the one thing mother most objects to is for Polly to wander off alone at night. She did it once when she was a very little girl."

"Don't worry, Mollie, she is sure to be back in half a minute when she remembers," the older woman replied.

CHAPTER XX

"POLLY"

But Polly did not come back within the hour or indeed all night. Naturally there was little sleep among the Camp Fire girls or their guardian who imagined all possible tragedies. Miss McMurtry wondered if Polly could have gone down to the lake and in the darkness fallen into the water, but then the moon was shining brilliantly and she could swim with perfect ease. This idea was only brought on by fear. What had probably happened was that she had wandered off for a walk, lost her way and decided that it was far wiser to spend the night quietly in the woods rather than wear herself out with tramping. When the sunrise came she would return.

With this idea Miss McMurtry comforted and encouraged the girls, for it was impossible that they should do more than search for their companion in the near-by woods and fields. It is true that Betty wanted to attempt to climb Sunrise Hill, taking lanterns with her, fearing that Polly had attempted a short walk and managed to sprain her ankle, and that Esther and Sylvia Wharton were more than anxious to go with her, but Miss McMurtry would not hear of it, having a vision of four lost girls instead of one. There was nothing to do but wait the few hours now until daybreak and then if Polly did not return, properly organize searching parties to seek for her. If the Camp Fire girls had learned anything of scouting methods, this would be their opportunity.

Mollie O'Neill was of course the person who required the tenderest care during the night. She and Polly were closer than other sisters, so unlike in temperament and yet one another's shadows. If only she could have imagined some explanation for her sister's disappearance, for of course everybody knew of Polly's sudden vagaries and yet it was unlike her to be so inconsiderate without cause.

Although Betty Ashton probably understood her friend even better than her sister did, as she sat quietly by Mollie's side for several hours insisting that there was really nothing alarming in Polly's flight and that she would doubtless be both vexed and ashamed of herself in the morning, she too was equally puzzled. For naturally she was not so confident as she pretended, although not until her hour came for rest and after she had actually tumbled into bed did she break down. Then Esther and Sylvia Wharton, who in some strange, quiet fashion seemed a comfort to everyone to-night, had insisted that they relieve Betty's watch with Mollie.

Dropping on her couch, not to sleep but to gain strength for the next day's quest, quite by accident Betty's hand slipped under her pillow. With a low exclamation, overheard by the other three girls in the tent, she drew out folded square of paper. Her name was on the outside, apparently hurriedly addressed in Polly's handwriting. It read:

DEAR BETTY:

Your money was stolen, at least not in the way you think it was, but perhaps in another almost as bad. For I found it in the woods on the day when I went into the village alone and I made no effort to find out to whom it belonged. You must have dropped it out of your letter on your way back to camp, for there was no mark on the envelope in which I found it. But I do not mean this as an excuse, I do not think it one. If I had not felt like a thief perhaps I would not have been ashamed to confess my fault before the other girls as I should have done before our altar fire to-night. I tried but I did not have the courage, so I am going away from camp. Please tell Miss McMurtry, Mollie and the other girls and do not ask me to come back, for it is impossible. If I could return your money, Betty, I should not feel so bitterly humiliated, but as I cannot at present I would rather not see you until I can. Of course we are no longer friends, for you cannot wish it, and always it has seemed to me that your wealth and my poverty makes the gulf between us. I can only say that I am truly sorry.

Yours sincerely,

POLLY

Having finished this ungracious note of apology Betty handed it without comment to Esther and then buried her own head in the pillow. If Polly could feel toward her in this manner because of a mistake which they had both made, then nothing she could do or say would make any difference. For to insist to Polly that she had a perfect right to use the money found by accident would not be altogether true and would not change her point of view, while to declare that the return of the money to its rightful owner was a matter of indifference would only deepen the misunderstanding.

Less accustomed to Polly's writing Esther read the note aloud slowly and then it was that Mollie's and Betty's positions were changed, and Mollie became instead of the comforted - the comforter.

"That is exactly like Polly O'Neill," she announced indignantly, "here she has done something she ought not to do without thinking, like spending that money without trying to find its owner, and now because she is so sorry she goes ahead and makes things worse for everybody instead of better." Mollie slid off her own hemlock bed and crossing the tent sat down by Betty. "Don't you worry, dear, or feel in the least responsible," she whispered, "you know Polly is hateful sometimes just because she is so ashamed and miserable she does not know how to be anything else. She does care for you more than anyone and you know that she will do almost anything to make peace with you as soon as she comes to her senses. Of course, Betty, I understand you don't care for the money part, why you would give either of us ten times that amount if you could and we would accept it, but you won't mind my writing mother to make things all right."

Then after a few words of explanation to their guardian the Camp Fire girls slept quietly until daylight, but even after they had eaten a hurried breakfast together the wanderer had not returned.

So immediately afterwards three parties set out, leaving Edith Norton and Juliet Field behind to protect the camp and to announce by the ringing of a bell if

Polly should return or if they were in any need.

Betty, Sylvia and Esther went off in one direction, Miss McMurtry and the two younger girls, Nan and Beatrice, in another, while Mollie, Meg and Eleanor took the interior of the Webster farm. The chief obstacle in their search being that it was apparently impossible to discover the direction of Polly's footprints on first leaving camp, the grass in the neighborhood being so constantly trodden down by the feet of so many girls.

Billy Webster, as he preferred to be called, was in a wheat field with his reaper just about to start to work, when a Camp Fire girl, whether Mollie or Polly he could not tell at first, came running toward him in apparent distress. So as not to make another mistake he let the girl speak first, only smiling at her in a sufficiently friendly fashion to make it very simple.

Mollie's first words were luminous. "Have you seen anything of Polly? She is lost or gone away or at least we can't find her!"

Therefore until lunch time Billy kept up the search over the farm with the three girls. And though they were not successful in making any discovery it was surprising what a comfort the girls found him, particularly Mollie, who seemed to depend on him as though he had been an old friend.

"I am sure there isn't the least reason to be seriously alarmed," he assured her half a dozen times with a curious understanding of Polly's character; "you see your sister has got a funny streak in her that makes her mighty interesting and mighty uncertain." (How angry

Polly would have been could she have heard him!) "She has got a lot to learn before she settles down."

By noon, finding his three companions nearly exhausted, the young man persuaded them to go up to the big, comfortable farmhouse, see his mother, have their luncheon and rest. And straightway on meeting her, Mrs. Webster took a liking to Mollie that was to last all the rest of her life.

During this time Betty, Esther and Sylvia were going slowly along the main path that led through the fields and finally on to the high road into the village. Miss McMurtry and her assistants were climbing Sunrise Hill.

But Sylvia Wharton was so tediously slow. About every five minutes she would stop and kneel down in the dirt, attempting to fit an old shoe of Polly's into any fresh track she happened to observe. The other two girls wandered off into bits of woods or meadows near by, calling and hunting, but Sylvia never went with them.

"There is no use," she explained, "Polly has gone straight into Woodford and because it was night had to take the regular path instead of going through the fields as she usually does."

Claiming to have exactly traced her footsteps Esther and Betty were still not convinced. "It is such a stupid idea, Sylvia," Betty argued, "for there isn't anybody in town now to whom Polly would go in the middle of the night, and besides she would be ashamed to let people know she had run away from camp."

Nevertheless Sylvia kept stolidly on and because her companions had nothing better to suggest they followed after her.

On the high road Sylvia, who would still creep like a tortoise, suddenly stooped down. The August dust was very thick along the way and wagons had already been traveling into town, and yet she picked up a string of red, white and blue beads, which surely were Polly's, since patriotism had been one of her chief studies during the summer.

It was also Sylvia's suggestion that led the little party of friends straight to Mrs. O'Neill's closed cottage. The doors and windows in front of the house were sealed, but Betty found the door of the old kitchen halfway open. And there inside on her mother's lounge lay Polly! She seemed to be almost asleep when the girls entered, but awakened immediately and in a wholly different frame of mind.

Realizing in the last few hours, when it was too late, how great an anxiety her disappearance must have caused, she wanted to go back to camp, to confess her fault and at least to persuade Betty to forgive her. Yet she dared not trust herself to go alone, for Polly's head was aching furiously, her face was hot and flushed and any attempt to walk made her sick and dizzy.

While Betty and Esther were discussing what had best be done, Polly having trusted herself wholly to their hands, neither of them noticed Sylvia Wharton's withdrawal.

When they did there was hardly time to comment upon it before she reappeared at the back door with her round face covered with dust and looking more freckled and homelier than ever.

"A carriage will be here in five minutes to take us to camp; I have ordered it," she announced.

Margaret Vandercook

CHAPTER XXI

THE END OF THE SUMMER CAMP

Good-by to summer, good-by, good-by, Good-by to summer

Esther's plaintive song ceased abruptly, for Betty Ashton leaning over suddenly put her hand to her lips. And at the same moment Meg Everett holding fast to Little Brother dropped down on the ground by the girls with one arm full of early goldenrod and Michaelmas daisies.

"No use to make Esther stop singing, it won't help matters, Betty, dear, the summer has gone," she exclaimed. "Little Brother and I have just seen quail whirring about in the underbrush. See I lay our autumn bouquet at your feet," and she tossed her flowers over to Betty. "Where is Miss McMurtry?"

Betty made a wry face. "Gone into town, if you please, to see about some books - school books. Oh, it wasn't because I didn't agree with Esther's song that I made her stop singing, it was because it was so dreadfully true that I felt at the moment I couldn't bear it. You are sorry too, aren't you, Nan?" she queried, turning to the girl on the other side of her who was sewing industriously on a soft blue cashmere frock, almost similar in color and texture to the one Betty had at this moment inside her trunk. The gown represented the complete restoration of peace between Nan and Betty. At first there had been some difficulty in persuading Nan to accept it, but after all Betty had been kinder than most of the other girls! Moreover, there had been many other expressions of apology in words and deeds that Nan had accepted and stored away in her heart.

"I just can't bear to think of it either," she replied slowly, letting her hands rest idly in her lap for a moment. "I guess you other girls can't ever know what these weeks in camp have been to me and what a lot I've learned. I hope I ain't going to forget it ever and Miss Martha says she is going to try to get them to let me come back to the High School. It will be all right if any one will trust me enough to give me work to do afternoons."

Before replying Esther Clark put several pine logs and a great bundle of pine cones on the fire around which she and her friends were seated, and the girls were quiet for a moment watching them sparkle and blaze.

"I expect I know, Nan, at least better than any one else," Esther answered finally, "for you see this is the first summer of my whole life that I haven't spent at the asylum scrubbing and cooking and nobody caring anything about my work except that I got it done. Work this summer has seemed like play, hasn't it? And I wouldn't be here, except for The Princess. I wonder if I shall ever be able to repay her?"

"Oh, wonder something else, Esther," Betty returned ungraciously, for references of this kind always made her uncomfortable. "Here comes Polly and Mollie and, of course Sylvia. Bee, will you go find Eleanor and Juliet and let us have tea here by the camp fire. Donna and Edith will probably be here before we finish. Suppose each one of us places a stick on the fire and while it burns make a good wish for the Sunrise Camp. Hello, Polly, yes Sylvia is perfectly right, you must not sit down on the ground without something under you, yes, and you must let her put that wrap over your shoulders, the sun will be going down pretty soon and then it will be quite cool."

Polly submitted to Sylvia's attentions none too graciously, but a moment later turned toward the: younger girl. "You are a trump, Sylvia," she murmured. "I am sure I don't know what I should have done without you these past two weeks while I will have been ill. It is funny how you should happen to know just what to do for people who are sick when you are so young!"

Sylvia sat stolidly down next the speaker. "I am going to be a trained nurse when I am old enough, that's why," she answered calmly, apparently not even observing the surprise of her companions. "You see if I thought I had sense enough I would try to be a doctor, but as I haven't I shall just take care of sick people. I have already learned a good many things this summer."

Polly whistled and several of the girls laughed. "I don't doubt it for a moment, Sylvia Wharton!" Polly exclaimed, "for heaven alone can tell what you do know! But it is absurd to talk about your being a nurse, when you will be the richest one of us, child, perhaps even richer than 'The Princess'."

There was no reply from Sylvia, only her lips shut tight and her chin looked oddly square and determined for a young girl. But then Sylvia looked like her father, who, one must remember, was a self-made man. And sometimes the daughter also inherits the traits of character that have made the father a success.

Eleanor and Juliet at this moment appearing with the tea things, the kettle was hung above the fire on an arrangement of three pronged sticks and not until tea was over did the girls or Betty remember her suggestion. Then she handed Polly a pine knot first. "Thrust this into the fire, Polly, dear, and make a parting wish for Sunrise Camp," Betty explained, "for a few days more you know, and we must fold our tents and say farewell to our summer."

Polly quickly thrust her torch into the hottest blaze. "I wish," she said at once, her cheeks hot from the closeness of the flames and from her own thoughts, "that everybody in Sunrise Camp would promise to forgive me for my foolish behavior two weeks ago and all the anxiety and trouble I caused. The camp has given me a new motto this summer that I shall at least try to live up to. It reads: 'Think first!'"

"Yes, and if you had only thought second and asked for your mail at the post office that day after finding Betty's money, Polly, you would have had your own fifty dollar prize for the best essay on 'A Summer Camp Fire in the Woods'," Mollie added in her usual practical fashion, and then she gave a little sigh of relief that the money had been paid back to Betty without troubling the mother still so far away.

"I wonder if Polly is going to be our genius as well as

Eleanor," Esther next suggested quietly, "every Camp Fire club is sure to turn out at least one extraordinary person and of course ours will have two or three." Then she blushed hotly in her old embarrassed, fashion, clasping her big hands closely together as Betty, half laughing at her own suggestion, whispered something in her ear.

Juliet Field wished the Sunrise Camp long life, and Meg that they might keep up their work together in town during the coming winter, Eleanor that they might spend the next summer together, and then Betty, happening quite by chance to observe a wistful expression on Nan's face, passed the fifth pine stick to her.

"Tell us what you are thinking of, Nan," she said, speaking with special friendliness to the one girl who had not had entirely fair treatment at their hands. "I have an idea you have something special on your mind."

Nan shook her head, although she did what was asked of her. "Oh no," she explained, "or at least I am afraid you will think my wish very silly. I was just wishing that we were not going back to the village but were going to spend our winter together amid the snows."

Nan's suggestion was so surprising that everybody stared at her for one, almost two minutes before Betty spoke.

"Very well, Nan, let's stay," she returned, as though making a perfectly ordinary remark. "I can't bear for Esther and me to have to go back alone to our great, empty house with mother and father away and no knowing when they may come back." (There was a catch in Betty's voice that her friends understood, for Mr. Ashton was again seriously ill and there was no hope of his returning to America at present.) "We can't live in our tents of course, but I don't know why we can't build a log cabin and somehow manage to get back and forth to school. When the snow comes we can use our big sled."

"You are quite mad, Betty Ashton; Esther, please tie a handkerchief around her lips before she makes us all equally so," Polly requested, "for there is no hope of our doing anything so impossible, as she suggests." And then because she caught an expression almost of agreement on her sister Mollie's face, Polly paused, almost overcome with surprise. Mollie, the sensible; Mollie, the practical - it was incredible.

"I don't see that Betty's idea is so foolish, for at least some of us might be able to live in camp this winter," Mollie thinking aloud as she talked. "For you see, the doctor has said that Polly must be out of doors as much as possible for the next year, and mother writes she would rather not come home at present if we can possibly get on without her, for there is something or other going on in Ireland that she has not explained to us, but she says if she can stay a few months longer it may make a difference in all our futures. I believe she would be glad to let us remain in Sunrise Camp for the winter if your mother and father are willing and we can make things comfortable, Betty," she concluded.

The mental conception of a group of girls living together in a winter's camp in the woods was evidently too surprising to be grasped all at once, for no one else at the moment had anything to say, and then Esther, glancing off across the fields where a soft September haze suggested the approach of the twilight, exclaimed. "See, there are Miss McMurtry and Edith returning from town. Let us give them our Camp Fire call to welcome them home."

"Wohelo for work, Wohelo for health, Wohelo for love!"

The ten voices carried the refrain far across the country and somehow the echo returning to them from Sunrise Hill brought with it the suggestion of even happier days to come.

The second volume in the Camp Fire Girls' Series will be called "The Camp Fire Girls Amid the Snows." In this book the history of the girls will be revealed under very different conditions. More than ever will their life be built around the fire which has always been the center of the home. Various important changes will take place in the circumstances of the leading characters and mysteries merely suggested in the first story will be developed in the second.

www.ingramcontent.com/pod-product-compliance
Lightning Source LLC
Chambersburg PA
CBHW051821170626
46807CB00003B/964